The Plot

Against

Roger Rider

Books by Julian Symons

FICTION

The Plot Against Roger Rider
The Players and the Game
The Man Who Lost His Wife
The Man Whose Dreams Came True
The Man Who Killed Himself
The Belting Inheritance
The End of Solomon Grundy
The Plain Man
The Progress of a Crime
The Pipe Dream
The Color of Murder
Bogue's Fortune
The Narrowing Circle
The Broken Penny
The Thirty-first of February
Bland Beginning

NONFICTION

Mortal Consequences

JULIAN SYMONS

The Plot
Against
Roger Rider

1817

HARPER & ROW, PUBLISHERS
New York, Evanston
San Francisco, London

A JOAN KAHN–HARPER NOVEL OF SUSPENSE

FIRST U.S. EDITION

Designed by C. Linda Dingler

Library of Congress Cataloging in Publication Data

Symons, Julian, 1912–
  The plot against Roger Rider.

  "A Joan Kahn-Harper novel of suspense."
  I. Title.
PZ3.S9927Pn3   [PR6037.Y5]   823'.9'12   73–4161
ISBN 0–06–014188–3

For Alan and Winifred Eden-Green

PART ONE || The Plot
Against
Geoffrey Paradine

1

You could say that the plot against Geoffrey Paradine started at the same time as the plot against Roger Rider. That would not be wrong, although it might be a little misleading. And you could start the story of both plots at several different points. The moment when Henry Princeton stepped off the plane at Heathrow, for instance. Or the day when John Burlington Summers told his landlady in Sydney that he was going to pursue his researches into the Russian royal family elsewhere, and left for Spain. One of the plots might be said to have started when Sheila Rider saw her father coming out of a teashop with a woman. Or you could say that the whole thing began when Amanda Rider took Geoffrey Paradine to bed. But upon the whole the best starting point is the warm July day when Roger Rider went to consult a private detective.

The sign on the door said *Geo. Hadley, Private Inquiry Agent, Discretion Assured.* The room was smallish, on the third floor of a decaying block off Fleet Street. It was almost filled by a chipped desk on which there were a lot of papers, a hatstand, some bookshelves, a filing cabinet, two chairs and a portable typewriter. At the back there was a sort of cupboard where the private inquiry agent made tea. His name was not Geo. Hadley, but Eric Coope. He had bought the business from Hadley five years earlier, and had retained the name partly because there was supposed to be some good will attached to it, and partly because his own name seemed to him absurd. The good will proved to be almost nonexistent, and Coope scratched a living which only just supported his wife and two children in Ealing.

Coope was a man of forty. His long face and lugubrious manner concealed a romantic heart. In his previous job as an insurance claims assessor he had uncovered half a dozen cases of fraud, decided that his talents were being wasted, and used his savings to buy the business from Hadley, a stout wheezing man in his sixties who wanted to retire. It had proved, however, that a private inquiry agent's life was less glamorous than that of a claims assessor. Most of Coope's business was dismally dull, but, like all romantics, he lived in hope.

It was the fifth of July. The man who came into Coope's coop was big and burly, with blunt reddish features and an air of authority. Coope, who prided himself on his powers of observation, thought: About fifty, good shoes, expensive suit, doesn't have to scratch for pennies, very likely got his own business. The man said, "Mr. Hadley?"

"Right." In the office Coope was Hadley. "What can I do for you?"

"Are you in a position to undertake an inquiry, and report to me direct?"

"That's what we're here for," Coope said heartily, although the plural was not justified. "At the moment I would be free to give a job my personal attention."

"I want a check on my wife's movements."

Coope nodded, and drew a sheet of paper toward him. "Your name?"

"Is it necessary for you to know that? I could come in to receive reports here."

"I must have it, I'm afraid. And if I'm going to watch her—"

"Of course, you'd know it. All right. The name is Rider, Roger Rider. The address is Flat C, 149 Bruton Street. I have a house in the country, but that needn't concern you. Report to me at my office, British Medical Subsidiaries, BMS House. I want to know where she goes, who she sees, all the time she's not with me. Monday to Friday. You needn't bother about weekends."

"A daily report?"

"Weekly will do. For two weeks. Mark it private."

"Of course." Coope named his usual terms of a tenner a day plus itemized expenses, and they were so readily accepted that he wished he had said fifteen. He said that it would be helpful to know what he was looking for, but the big man replied that that was not in the agreement. He spoke throughout with a briskness that impressed Coope.

Another wife having a bit on the side, Coope thought; they're all the same nowadays. It wasn't a romantic assignment, but it was a week's work, probably more. He made a call to a friend in the library of a daily paper, learned that Rider was the chairman of BMS, and wished even more that he had pushed the fee higher.

The report was badly typed. Coope had taught himself touch typing, with unfortunate results. Only two of the items interested Rider.

Tuesday July 9   Subject left flat 12:30 P.M. Taxi to Mirabelle restaurant. Left 2:15 P.M. Ascertained subject lunched with Mrs. Page, fashion editor of *Beauty* magazine. Subject took taxi to Harrod's, arrived 2:30 P.M. Met in Harrod's short dark man aged 45 to 55, dark gray suit. Went out at once, taxi to flat in Bruton Street, paid off by him. Went in together 2:50 P.M. Man came out at 3:45 P.M. Subject did not reappear.

The other entry was for Friday, July 12. The short dark man's arrival at the flat that day had been at 3 P.M. He left at 3:55.

Rider read these entries without any particular expression on his heavy features. Then he rang up Coope, and said he wanted to know the name of the man.

"Naturally, Mr. Rider. And further reports on the subject's movements, no doubt."

"No further reports."

Coope coughed. "If you think of taking the matter further, it might be wise to arrange for another operator to—"

"I said, no further reports. Thank you. Just the name."

A couple of days later he received a memorandum from Coope. It said: "Subject's visitor is Geoffrey Paradine. Address: 33 Malbite Street, N.W. 5. Further information can be supplied if required."

Rider telephoned Coope, and said that the inquiry was now terminated.

"I hope our services have been satisfactory?"

"Perfectly. Let me have your account. I'll send a check."

It had been a humdrum little inquiry, but there were two reasons why Coope did not forget it. One was that the check Rider sent him was for fifty pounds more than the sum of his account. The other was the fact that Geoffrey Paradine was Foreign Sales Manager in Rider's own organization, BMS. I'd like to have seen his face when he read that name, Coope thought.

He would have thought this even more strongly if he had known that Geoffrey Paradine was not only an employee of Roger Rider, but also his oldest friend.

2

In its beginning the relationship between Billy Rider and Geoff Paradine was one found in almost any single-sex school, whether it is comprehensive, grammar or public. A big boy protects one who is smaller and often younger. He punches and kicks the small boy's persecutors, walks home with him, sometimes helps him with lessons or homework. The relationship between the two may be overtly sexual, particularly in a public school, or, on the surface at least, it may have nothing to do with sex. The Rider-Paradine friendship was of the second kind. If anybody had said to Billy that he had a sex thing going with

Geoff, he would have been answered by a mouthful of bad language. If the same thing had been said to Geoff, he would not have known what was meant.

They both lived in Kentish Town's dingy but respectable Malbite Street, and went to the secondary modern. Big Billy used to call every morning for little Geoff, go with him to school and come back with him in the afternoon. In the playground Billy protected Geoff from the fearsome Grant Street lot, who had it in for anyone from Malbite. One day Geoff ran home crying, to say that some boys had tried to beat him up. He was not hurt, however, so what had happened? With eyes cast down he said that Billy was fighting them, and had told him to run home. Billy ended up in the hospital with a fractured jaw. Geoff's father, who worked in a local ironmonger's, said that he had never expected to have a bleeding coward for a son, but his mother replied that Geoff couldn't be expected to stand up to those louts, and that while she was grateful to Billy for helping, he was just a lout too. Billy's father, a docker, had been killed in an accident at work when he was four. What his mother said is not known, but it would not have mattered, for Billy already went his own way.

At that time Billy was thirteen and Geoff eleven, and Geoff had already got in the way of doing what Billy told him. Life was so much easier that way. But it should not be assumed that he liked it. Who, after all, does like the subjection of his own personality to that of another? This is especially so when the subjected person is more intelligent than his dominator, and Geoff believed this, although there was no proof of it.

When the war came, Billy was twenty and Geoff eighteen. Billy was selling things off stalls in street markets, stuff that, as he said with a wink, he had picked up cheap. Geoff was in a white-collar job, an insurance clerk. Both were conscripted immediately. Billy had a good war, once he had latched on to the idea that promotion was connected with the tone in which you spoke, and the way in which you handled a knife and fork. He saw service in Africa, Italy and France, and ended up an infantry major. He also ended called Roger by all his brother officers, a name which referred to his exploits with girls. Geoff had a fairly miserable war, which he began and ended as an infantry private. He was graded B1 because of an ear defect, and never left England. He had always been good at chess, and the single achievement of his army career was to become regimental champion.

During the war, Roger (who never went back to Billy) and Geoffrey haven't seen much of each other, but once out of khaki they both return to Malbite Street. Their friendship is resumed, they go out on dates with girls together, in particular with two sisters named Mary and Paula Paine. Mary is the pretty one, Paula is sweet but plainish. Both the girls really want Roger, but it is Mary who gets him. There is a double wedding in church, which makes the local papers and even one or two nationals, because Roger's mother dies of a heart attack at the reception. By this time Roger is ready to leave Kentish Town.

In civvy street he got a job selling kitchen equipment, borrowed some money and started his own firm, selling a revolutionary new kitchen scouring pad. The pad was a success, Roger borrowed more money on the strength of it, bought a bigger firm that was on the skids, smartened up the look and widened the range of its products, made a success of that too. He was set to spread his wings and fly, up and away out of Kentish Town, to a house facing Regent's Park.

Geoffrey, in the meantime, has been living rather miserably, doing one job after another—bookshop assistant, journalist on a small weekly paper. His parents die suddenly, within a year of each other, leaving him the house in Malbite Street and a little money. He settles down in the house with Paula, puts most of the money into a theater project which collapses almost immediately. Geoffrey has vague artistic aspirations, and is writing a novel. He is still good at chess, and plays a great deal.

At this stage the Paradines don't see much of the Riders. Both have produced children. James, the son of Geoffrey and Paula, is born a couple of years before Sheila Rider. But it should not be thought that Roger Rider forgot his old friend and follower. At Christmas, presents are always exchanged in person. Sometimes Roger and Mary bring little Sheila to Malbite Street. Gifts, as it seems dozens of them, are disgorged from the Bentley, Roger brings wonderful crackers containing hats, false noses and indoor fireworks, and is uproariously cheerful. Little James loves him, but it is noticeable that Paula becomes increasingly tight-lipped as the day goes on, and sharply slaps away Roger's hand when he puts it round her waist. Sometimes the Paradines visit the Regent's Park palazzo, where Roger carves the turkey, but a flunky stands round to serve the chateau-bottled claret which the master of the house sniffs and tastes knowingly, before roaring with laughter and saying that all he knows about drink is how to pour it down his gullet.

When they come away one year Paula says, "Thank God that's over." Geoffrey agrees, and she bursts out, "He's supposed to be your friend. If you don't like it either, what's the point of going? I'd sooner stay at home in our slum."

"Is that what you call it? It was good enough for my mother and father. And you didn't live so far away."

"I'm sorry. But you must see what I mean."

"And she's your sister. But you never have liked Roger."

"I don't like his attitude to you, that's all."

They would bicker like this for half an hour. But while the children were small, Christmas visits were still exchanged, with occasional picnics and children's parties.

In the next ten years certain incidents occurred that fixed forever the pattern of the Rider-Paradine relationship.

When Sheila was five years old, Mary left Roger, taking the little girl with her. She went off with the managing director of an Italian chemical firm, who was in London trying to do a deal with Roger about handling its products. It was typical of Roger that he should not have allowed her departure to interfere with the deal being carried through, typical of him also that he should have fought for and obtained the return of Sheila. At this time he saw Paula and Geoffrey often, coming round to the little house in Malbite Street for supper, talking about old times. Paula asked him whether Sheila might not be better off with her mother. "That bitch. Begging your pardon, Paula love, I know she's your sister, but it's true. What could she have wanted, anyway, that I didn't give her? Anything she wanted, she could buy." "Except you. She told me she saw you an hour a day, morning and evening. Plus bed, she said there was always that." Roger ignored this. "She was a bitch. If she wanted to go and get herself shagged by a spaghetti eater, all right. She can have a divorce, I won't argue about money within reason. But she's not taking my daughter. Sheila belongs to me."

So there was a divorce. Sheila came back, was brought up by a governess for a year or two, then went to boarding school and saw very little of her father. There was plenty of money, because Roger's affairs expanded and expanded. He bought a baby-foods firm, then the Bollit and Pangborne chain of chemists, then BMS —British Medical Subsidiaries—itself. He had long since gone public, of course, and when he bought BMS there were murmurs about the Monopoly Commission, but they came to nothing. So Roger moved on and on and up and up, like the shares in his companies, away out of Regent's Park to a manor house in Sussex and a flat in Mayfair. He hobnobbed with industrialists and with politicians of both parties; bankers asked his views about sterling and the dollar. But still Roger did not forget his oldest friend, Geoff, who was now a badly paid editor working for a group that ran a series of technical papers.

Item. Geoffrey's first and only novel, *Human Feelings*, is published. It receives six reviews, three of them friendly, sells just over 600 copies. Geoffrey discovers from the publishers that Roger has bought 250 of these and given them away to friends.

Item. Two years after Mary leaves Roger, Geoffrey returns home early one day with a migraine headache, and finds his wife in bed with his oldest friend. It is typical of Roger, again, that he tries to convince Geoffrey that what has happened is of no importance.

10

"I'm not a great reader, Geoff, you know that, but I'll tell you something a great writer said about it. H. G. Wells. He said it was no more important than sneezing."

Geoffrey sat with his hands clasped together, his eyes looking at the floor, in the little sitting room. He very rarely gave way to emotion. "Go away."

"Honestly, Geoff, I'm sorry. But don't make too much of it."

With hands clenched into fists, Geoffrey repeated: "Go away."

Roger went away. Soon after Paula came downstairs James returned from school. When he had gone to bed, Paula said, "Aren't you going to say something? You must have known I was always a bit in love with him."

"No."

"What do you mean, no?"

"I didn't know. But I don't see that there is anything to say."

"You come home and find me in bed with Roger, and there's nothing to say? Didn't you have a row with him? You must know he took me to bed because I belonged to you, not because he was mad about a housewife. And because he'd lost Mary too—that was something to do with it. He doesn't like losing things. You know all that, why didn't you say any of it?"

"What would have been the point?"

"The point! For God's sake, what are you? Why don't you shout, why don't you hit me? You write a book about human feelings, but you don't have any yourself. No wonder nobody would buy it."

Without raising his voice Geoffrey Paradine said, "Oh, yes, I have human feelings."

Then he went upstairs to the little room he used as a study, where a game of chess played by the masters was always set up, for him to replay and brood over. There was a bed in the room too, and that night he slept in it.

The next day Geoffrey Paradine did something he had never done before. When he left the office he walked home to Kentish Town, having a drink in every pub on the way. He arrived not, as usual, at a quarter to seven but at nine o'clock, and although still able to stand up, he was very drunk. It took a few moments for him to understand the meaning of the smell of gas that met him in the hall.

Paula had done the classical thing. She had arranged for James to spend the evening with a neighbor, turned on the gas oven after sealing the windows and door with tape, and then put her head on a cushion beside it. The coroner did not mention the point at the inquest, but Geoffrey worked out that if he had come home at the usual time Paula's life might have been saved. It was possible, that like many people who attempt suicide, she was really calling out for help.

Roger did not come to the funeral, but he sent the biggest wreath.

Afterward Geoffrey Paradine, a small hunched withdrawn man, went on living in Malbite Street with his son. He got a woman in to do some cleaning and to bring James home from school, but otherwise looked after the boy himself. It was six months after Paula's death that Roger's Bentley came again to Malbite Street.

When Geoffrey opened the door, Roger flung out his arms. "Geoff," he said. When Geoffrey made no move, he dropped them dramatically at his sides. "Are you going to say I can't come in?"

For Geoffrey Paradine there was always something mesmerically compelling about Roger Rider. He stood aside.

Roger's big body filled the sitting room. He stood looking round. "You haven't changed things much."

"Not much."

"How's the boy?"

"All right. He's out playing."

"I didn't come to the funeral, thought you wouldn't want it." He looked round again. "Haven't got a drink, Geoff, I suppose?"

Geoffrey went to a cupboard, took out a bottle and two glasses. "It's cheap sherry, not chateau-bottled claret."

"The boy's at the primary, I suppose."

"That's right. The one we went to."

"Geoff." Roger drank his sherry at a gulp, poured another glass. "No use talking about the past, saying I'm sorry. Agreed?" There was no reply. "I'm in a fix, Geoff. I've had to sack two department heads who were plotting against me. I need an honest man." He drained the second glass, shuddering slightly. "Geoff, come and work with me."

In his flat voice Geoffrey Paradine said, "Blood money. Payment for Paula."

"If anybody else said that, I wouldn't take it. But listen to me, Geoff, just listen, that's all I ask. I want someone I can depend on, someone I can talk to, as assistant in Foreign Sales. Now, don't tell me you couldn't do the work. Anyone who can do that editorial job with the stinking lot who employ you now could do this standing on his head. I don't know what you're getting—"

Geoffrey told him. It was not much. Roger said that he would double it, and that that was only a start.

It is possible that Geoffrey might have refused, if James had not chosen that moment to come home. As the boy, fresh-faced and cheerful, greeted the man he called Uncle Roger, it came home to Geoffrey that the money could mean a lot to his son. It meant the chance of going to a good boarding school, of getting away from a father who did little in the evenings but play chess and read Dostoevsky. Those were his conscious thoughts. It occurred to him afterward that his unconscious ones perhaps contained the desire to be again some kind of subordinate to Roger. He said that he would think about it, and then he said yes.

Within a year he had been promoted to Foreign Sales Manager, doing work in which he had no interest, and which he did not fully understand. James went to that good boarding school, came home on holidays, got a scholarship to a university. Geoffrey stayed in Malbite Street, now looked after by a housekeeper who sometimes infuriated him by moving his chess pieces from their positions on the board. He saw Roger little outside the business.

And fifteen years after he joined BMS he went to bed with Roger's second wife, Amanda.

3

Every Wednesday Geoffrey took nearly three hours for lunch. He might have taken long lunch hours on other days if he had wished, since most of the work in the department was done by a competent young man named Neasden, but he rarely took more than a few minutes over the statutory hour. On Wednesdays, however, he went to the Staunton Chess Club in the City, where he was a known and respected figure. Several of the best players in London used the Staunton, and he played a game against one of them. Unusually, he preferred the black pieces, for his ambition was to perfect a new defensive gambit, which he hoped would one day be known as Paradine's Defense. Most of the games in which he played it ended in a draw, but he was hopeful that he would eventually be able to evolve a successful attacking position from it.

On this particular Wednesday, June 12, his attempt to move out of defense into attack had ended in defeat, and he was not in the best of tempers when he hailed a taxi. As it pulled up he heard with astonishment a woman's voice say, "Mine." He responded snappishly that he had called the taxi first, and turned to see Amanda Rider. They had met only at a few BMS official functions, but he recognized her.

"Mr. Paradine, isn't it? Are you going back to the office? Why don't we share a taxi, and you can drop me off at my flat, Bruton Street."

Sitting in the taxi beside Amanda Rider, he was aware of her as he had not been on other occasions. He knew almost nothing about her, except that Roger had married her five years ago, that she was said to have been an actress, and that she was not much more than half Roger's age. She was dark, with a pale skin, slender and not very tall. She had blue eyes, and a voice as cool as water. The things she said in this cool unaccented voice seemed to have more than their obvious meaning, as she told him that Roger had spoken about him often, said that they should see him more often, he must come to dinner, stay a weekend at Pevering Manor. Just before they reached the flat she said, "I almost forgot. There are some papers Roger wants at the office. Would you mind picking them up?"

In the vestibule she said that she had left a scarf in the taxi, and ran back to get it. Then they were in the flat, which contained chairs that looked like soap bubbles, tables made of glass, or plexiglass, one long wall that seemed to be covered with torn black foam rubber hanging down in strips.

"Do you like it? No need to answer, I can see you don't. I'm not sure that I do much, though it seemed a good idea at the time."

"What about Roger?"

"He'd hardly notice. Anyway, he lets me do what I like. What do you think about me?" He found the question impossible to answer. "I think you're dishy."

She was standing close, without actually touching him. Suddenly she said in a mock-Cockney voice, so different that for a moment he was startled: "So 'ow about it, ducks, aintcher goin' to leave a girl any of 'er pride?"

She took hold of his hand now, and led him toward the bedroom. By the door she said, in a sort of mock Old English: "Would't be sacrilege to soil thy boss's sheets? There's always the spare room. Or the floor."

"Your husband's sheets."

"The sheets of your oldest friend. All right, the spare room it is."

He thought of something. "The taxi. He'll be waiting."

"Wouldn't it be worth the extra fare?" She laughed. "Don't worry, I paid him off."

"The scarf."

"The imaginary scarf."

It was months since he had had a woman, and then it had been a brief unsatisfactory encounter with a prostitute. He did not feel that he acquitted himself well. When it was over, she smiled and said, "Now you can say you've been to bed with the wife of your oldest friend." For a moment he wondered whether she knew about Paula, then dismissed the thought.

At the office he said that he had a migraine, and went home. He put out the pieces to replay the last few moves of the game he had lost at lunchtime but found it impossible to concentrate. What had happened seemed unbelievable. Perhaps he had imagined it all. He could not even remember what her face looked like. It occurred to him that she was perhaps what is called a nymphomaniac. If so, it was interesting to have met one, but he would not want to repeat the experience. Yet it stayed with him. The taste of her seemed to flavor the next day's food, and he found himself trying to summon up the picture of her unremembered face while he was looking at letters in the office.

On Friday, just before lunch, the telephone rang. A woman's voice, very businesslike, said, "This is the British Blood Sports League. The rabbit you ordered is ready."

"Rabbit?"

"It's skinned, waiting for your collection." He was about to say that there must be some mistake when Amanda's voice, cool and unemphatic, said, "Three o'clock. Don't be late."

He went to the flat. He told himself that he wanted to find out what she looked like, what made her tick, but in truth it would have been impossible for him not to have gone. Afterward she lay on the bed and smoked. She said, "Not had too much experience, have you?"

"Not recently. I'm sorry."

"It doesn't matter. Rather interesting, really."

He was trying to imprint her face and body on his mind, so that he would not forget again. The eyes now seemed greenish rather than blue, the face was delicate, finely drawn, triangular, the body boyish with small breasts, the nipples no more than dark pimples. He was aware of being in a thrall that he had no wish to escape, yet he could not resist asking the question that might break it.

"Why me? I mean, I'm sure you could get somebody—better. Or younger."

She blew the smoke upward in a perfect ring before saying in mock-Cockney: "Carn't yer take yes for an arnswer then; 'ave I got to beg for it?" Then in her usual voice: "Roger."

"What about him?"

"There might be somebody else. They wouldn't work for Roger. Or know him like you do."

"You're doing this just to get back at him over something?" It was absurd that he should feel disappointed, that he should have hoped for anything else, but he knew now that he had. Full of shame and indignation, he scrambled off the bed, feeling ridiculous because of his nakedness, and began to dress. "You must hate him."

She asked with amusement, "Don't you?"

He realized then that she did know about Paula. He left swearing to himself that he would never go there again, that this was the end.

It was not, however, the end but the beginning. When she rang up a few days later to say in Brooklynese that baby was waiting for poppa, he put down the telephone; but her next call, made in broken French to say that he was expected at Madame Gamarouche's salon, undid him. After that there was no turning back. They met twice a week, always after a telephone call that she made to the office. She never rang him at home, and said that he was never to ring her. Sometimes they met in the banking hall at Harrod's, sometimes he went straight to the flat. Her manner at their meetings was so much at variance with the coolly languid personality she presented to the world that he sometimes suspected her of being on drugs, but he saw no sign that this was true. He did not flatter himself that even with what might be called her training he became a particularly skillful lover. It seemed to him that her hatred of Roger must be intense.

Of more concern to him were his own emotions. He told himself that it was not possible to love such a woman, a woman who apparently found sex intensely exciting while being quite unmoved by it emotionally (he remembered those words said long ago about it being no more important than a sneeze), yet there could be no doubt that he was obsessed by her. His chess game declined, his appetite slackened, Mrs. Merchant reproached him with not doing justice to her breaded cutlets and steak-and-kidney pie. Dostoevsky seemed to provide no answer to his situation, nor did *Madame Bovary* when he reread it, nor did Proust. He tried to believe that his actions were based on a simple desire for revenge against Roger, but he knew that this was not true. He began to read poetry again, and learned by heart Keats's "La Belle Dame sans Merci" and bits of Swinburne. Could it be that what he felt was love? It was certainly unlike any emotion that he had known before.

4

Ten days after receiving Coope's report, Roger Rider tried to get hold of Geoffrey in the office, and was told by an apologetic Neasden that he was out. Roger left a message. Neasden made a mental note that the Chairman had tried a couple of times before to get hold of Paradine in the afternoon without success. Perhaps storms were on the way? If so, they could surely mean nothing but good for an enterprising assistant to an inefficient department head.

Roger looked at his watch. The time was four fifteen. He asked Dick Taylor to come in.

Taylor, an amiable moon-face whose chief aim in life was the avoidance of trouble, was the General Manager. He liked people to be happy and friendly, and usually the Chairman was both. But not today.

"The Foreign Sales Department. What's your feeling about the way it's being run?"

Taylor immediately looked, and indeed felt, concerned. He had no wish to say anything at all about the Foreign Sales Department, in which the Chairman himself had always taken a close interest. Fortunately, Rider went on talking, so that he was saved from the responsibility of an instant reply.

"I've just tried to get Geoffrey Paradine. He's out. This is the third time in the last fortnight that he's been out at four in the afternoon. You've no idea where he is?"

"I'm afraid not." Taylor injected a note of regret into the words, although he might have said that Paradine was a department head, and that the General Manager was not his keeper.

"I'm not happy with the way Foreign Sales is being run. What about Neasden?"

"A very efficient young man."

"Geoffrey Paradine is one of my oldest friends. What do you think of his work, Dick? You can be frank with me, you know that."

What an appalling question! There was nothing that Taylor disliked more than having to express a positive opinion to a superior without knowing quite what that superior expected to hear. His true opinion would have been that Paradine had never been up to the job at all, but that could hardly be the right thing to say. "To be candid—" He paused.

"Yes?"

"He doesn't seem quite on top of the job lately." The Chairman nodded. Taylor went on. "Perhaps he has some personal problem."

"It's difficult for me. As an old friend." With apparent irrelevance he continued. "I'm going to Spain on holiday at the beginning of September. To the villa."

Taylor brightened. Perhaps the worst was over, they could have a chat about holiday plans. "We're off to Norway. Marvelous fishing."

"I thought of inviting Paradine. He lives alone, you know. And we're very old friends. I hoped we might get whatever it is straightened out."

Taylor beamed. His course was now set fair. "Marvelous idea." "The firm must be put first, of course, but I shouldn't like to lose Geoffrey. If he's got something on his mind—he's a terrible worrier, always was—there's nothing like a little relaxation in the sun to make you talk about it. You don't think I'm imagining things? About his work, I mean. . . . I'm glad of that, Dick. And many thanks for your help."

A quarter of an hour later Geoffrey came in to see him. "That was a long lunch," Roger said genially. "I tried to get you just after four."

"I'm sorry. I played chess at the club, and the game took longer than we expected. Neither of us would agree to a draw."

"You won, I hope? Yes, I can see you did." A smile, brief as a lightning flash, had appeared on Geoffrey's lips. "Never mind about that. You know the villa?" He did not wait for a reply. The BMS villa, at which the directors and selected guests spent their holidays, was known to all executive staff. "I'm going out at the beginning of September, for a month probably. Come with me. Do you good. You've been looking under the weather lately. I'm not sure it isn't affecting your work." Again that flicker of a smile. "Just a small party, Amanda and myself. And my daughter —you remember Sheila—I'm asking her. What about your boy, what's he doing? Delighted to have him along as well."

"I don't know," Geoffrey said slowly. "Thank you for the invitation, Roger, but I don't know."

"Nonsense. You never were any good at making up your mind. I'll do it for you: you're coming. There are things about the running of the department that worry me. I want to talk to you about them. And I need somebody I can relax with, Geoff. We'll talk about old times and the things we got up to when we were boys, eh?"

In his mind's eye Geoffrey saw himself walking along a silvery beach with Amanda, swimming naked with her in a pool, taking long walks among mountains, walks during which no words were spoken, an occasional smile from one to the other showing how perfectly they were in tune. He knew that these were improbable fictions, but his mind dwelt on them. Two or three weeks earlier he would have thought that he was betraying his host. Now he barely thought about Roger at all. He said that he would like to come.

His acceptance forged another link in the chain of the plot against Roger Rider.

5

Since Sheila Rider had insisted on leaving school when she was sixteen, saying that she wanted to earn her own living, she saw her father no more than three or four times a year. There would be the sudden swoop on the flat in Chiswick, which she shared with two other girls, to carry her off to dinner, and once a year a weekend at Pevering Manor, and that was about all. That, to be truthful, was all she wanted. She had no interest in the kind of life her father lived or the things he did, she disliked her stepmother, she was perfectly happy as an art teacher in a grammar school. Perhaps it was an exaggeration to say perfectly happy, because she would have liked to be an artist, and the feeble little water colors and abstracts she produced had convinced her that there was no hope of this.

There was also, if one talked about perfect happiness, the question of the missing man. Sheila had had in mind since her schooldays the image not exactly of a *perfect* but of a Natural Man, one who would have as little time as she for the artificialities of the civilization they lived in. Sheila acknowledged that she lived in it too, but she knew that when the Natural Man arrived she would gladly join with him in some simpler and superior way of living. The schoolmasters and others who had, as it were, made application for this position had proved far from satisfactory. Their eyes lit up at mention of Natural Man, but their subsequent actions showed that they interpreted her meaning quite wrongly.

But still, she was always pleased to hear her father's booming voice. Her affection for him was genuine, although it might not have survived seeing too much of him. She said this when he extended the invitation. She was a girl who liked to speak her mind.

"It sounds nice, but—a whole month in Spain. Do you think I should survive that long? With Amanda there too?"

His laugh, loud and unaffected, came down the line. "If you can't stand your old man you can always clear out after a few days, no offense taken. I tell you who else is coming—Geoff Paradine, you remember him. And I'm asking his son, that's your cousin James. Very promising lad, I'm told, very intellectual, just suit you."

"Most unlikely." She thought of something. "And talking about unlikely things, who was that girl I saw you with the other day? Coming out of a teashop, of all places. I could hardly believe my eyes."

He guffawed. "My latest mistress. You'll come, then?"

She and one of her flat mates had planned a holiday in the Dordogne which had fallen through. She was not going anywhere, and the holiday would be free. She said yes.

After he had rung off, she thought again about the curious little incident. She had been walking down Holborn, a couple of weeks earlier, and had seen her father coming out of a dismal-looking little café with a small, quite unremarkable young woman. She had shown surprise, because it was not the kind of place she would have expected him to be seen dead in, to use the old phrase. He had looked embarrassed, which was unusual, and what he said by way of explanation seemed ridiculous. However, it was even more absurd to think of the girl as his mistress. What *had* he been doing in a dingy teashop? She made up her mind to ask him when they were out in Spain.

6

James Paradine and Jerry Maitland sat at the table in the sitting room of the small flat they shared, playing piquet. James looked across at Jerry's bullet head, smooth apple cheeks and curly black hair, and wondered again about the problem that had been occupying him for months. Am I queer, he wondered, or not?

It was a worrying question, or rather it had become worrying soon after he began to share a flat with Jerry. Of course he knew that in theory we are all bi-sexual, and that we all have secondary sexual characteristics, the incipient mustaches of women, the swelling breasts of some men. When a prefect at boarding school had told him that he looked like Rupert Brooke, he knew that this was a preliminary to a sexual advance, and he had noticed that he felt the same excitement at the touch of a boy's hand and a girl's. But that had been at boarding school, where everybody had homosexual experiences. At the new, fashionable university he went to, he had bedded a variety of girls but had never felt any inclination to make approaches to a man. Yet there could be no doubt of his desire to embrace Jerry at times, nor that the sight of Jerry coming naked out of the bath roused in him what could only be called sexual feelings. At the same time his desire to get girls into bed seemed not to be quite what it had been. He had not mentioned all this to Jerry, because his friend was emphatically heterosexual, but the whole thing was worrying.

It was made more worrying, and also slightly ridiculous, by the fact that Jerry was a sergeant in Scotland Yard's Fraud Squad. They had met at a soccer match, when James had been playing for his university, and Jerry for a Metropolitan Police team. Jerry had tackled him savagely from behind, had apologized after the game and then bought him a drink. Over the drink they had discovered that they were both looking for somewhere to live, and when a week later Jerry rang to say that he had found a flat off Gray's Inn Road at an extremely reasonable rent, James accepted immediately his offer to share it. Perhaps it had been a mistake to share a flat with a policeman? Certainly it was if one nursed amorous feelings, but at the time it had seemed an idea that must be helpful in relation to James's postgraduate thesis on "Interconnections Between Real-Life Crime and Crime Literature."

If one continued this line of reasoning, there was no legal reason why a copper shouldn't be a consenting homosexual adult, but somehow the idea was comic. It was especially comic in relation to bullet-headed Jerry, who sat opposite him now, characteristically chewing the end of a pencil while he made up his mind which cards to get rid of. He could leave the flat, but that would just be postponing the problem, not solving it. To admit that he was bi-sexual seemed somehow unsatisfactory—he didn't actually *feel* bi-sexual, simply unusually affectionate toward Jerry. What other solution was there? Cold baths?

Jerry discarded. James had the elder hand. "Point six," he said.
"Good."
"Sequence five."
"Equal."
"Ace high."
"Good."
"And I have a quatorze. Of kings."

Jerry was busy with his pencil. "That's a repique. Ninety-five points to nothing." They played the hand. Jerry made one trick out of the twelve. "Last hand and I'm rubiconed. You lucky old sod."

It was at this moment that Roger Rider rang up. James had not seen him for years, yet he recognized the confident voice as it echoed down the line. Roger told him that his father was going to Spain.

"Do you see much of your dad these days?"

A mild twinge of guilt. "I go over every few days. He's usually pretty much wrapped up in a chess problem. I sometimes think he finds it hard to distinguish me from one of the pieces."

"I'm a bit worried about him. It'll do him good to get away, relax. I know he'd like it if you came too, but he asked me to ring. Your cousin's coming too—Sheila, remember her?"

"Of course. I haven't seen her since she was—oh, fourteen, I suppose."

"Pretty girl. You'll like her. What do you say?"

In the back of James's mind there had been a pipe dream about going on a walking tour in the Highlands with Jerry. Together they strode up the hills, sang in pubs each evening while they drank whisky with a beer chaser. And afterward—

"Mawkish," he said.

"What's that?"

"Sorry. I'd love to come." Perhaps a pretty girl was just what he needed. He was quite unprepared for Jerry's reaction when James told him who had telephoned.

"Rider? The BMS man?"

"Yes. He's an old friend of my father's. Schoolboys together, always been friends since. He gave dad the job at BMS."

"And you're going to be in Spain with him when? Beginning of September." Jerry chewed his pencil thoughtfully. "Write to me, will you?"

"Send a postcard, you mean?"

"No, I mean letters. About what goes on, but especially about Rider. What he's like, what he does, everything. It means something, boy, or it could mean something. I wouldn't ask otherwise."

"Do you mean there's something wrong with him?"

"Can't tell you any more. I daresay there's nothing to any of it, but it might be a lot of help. To me." Jerry looked directly at him. The idea of writing letters was attractive, the appeal of his look irresistible.

"All right. Don't expect too much, though. I don't remember him as a wildly exciting character. Forceful but humdrum, I'd say." His mind moved back to thoughts of a few minutes earlier. "This flat, Jerry. You must have leaned on somebody to get it so cheap."

Jerry's smile was that of a naughty schoolboy. "Let's say somebody owed me a favor."

"Why didn't you get another copper to go in with you?"

"Most policemen are such boring bastards, that's why. Girls and booze, that's all they think about."

"You're a right one to complain about that. What's happened to the girl you were telling me about, the one who couldn't get enough of it?"

"Gone the way of all flesh." Jerry grinned. "I don't have anything against girls or booze, right. But the rest of the time they talk about the job, and I can't take that." He grinned again. "Now, with you I knew I'd get a high class of conversation, even though it's mostly crap."

"I thought you agreed that Buñuel film was terrific."

"I was talking about the girl in it, cock, I thought you understood that. The one who hired herself out in a brothel. Which reminds me, I've got a date with a bird. You know the old saying, never keep a bird in the hand waiting if you want to end up in her bush. By the way, what I said about Rider, keep it under your hat. Chances are it's all nothing. If it's all cleared up before you go out on holiday, I'll let you know."

But when James asked the night before departure whether Jerry still wanted him to write letters, the answer was yes.

7

Jerry Maitland had been apprenticed to a firm of accountants for three years when he decided that the life ahead of him would be unendurably boring. It was by chance that he joined the police rather than the army, but once in the police it was almost inevitable that he should graduate to the Fraud Squad.

Just after the war it was realized that it might be a good idea to create at Scotland Yard a department which would concentrate on the investigation of complicated commercial frauds. The result was the semi-autonomous Department C6, the Fraud Squad. Its members, who are not qualified accountants but possess or develop a nose for fraud, operate mostly in London, but may be called in to unravel tangled skeins in the provinces. It had often occurred to Jerry that the money he got was a small fraction of what he would have earned as a practicing chartered accountant, and he sometimes thought that checking figures was a bookkeeper's job and not a policeman's, and that it was equally unexciting whether you were doing it in London, Birmingham or Bournemouth. Inside C6 he worked in a team with Charlie Featherstone.

Detective Chief Superintendent Featherstone, who was naturally called Feathers, had the red face, broad shoulders and big hard belly of many policemen. He was, indeed, a hard man with, in Jerry's view, a limited imagination. He was also a cautious man, not prone to excitement or enthusiasm, and now that he was a couple of years away from retirement, perhaps his caution had grown. There had been a time when he was eager to get his teeth into a company's books, but nowadays he seemed to the sergeant only to want to coast into harbor. He was distinctly lukewarm about the question of Roger Rider.

"Oh ah," he said, when Maitland told him of his arrangement for learning about Rider's movements on holiday from a friend. "Why are we worrying about this character at all, tell me that. A query from the Board of Trade or Customs, was it?"

"No, sir. It was a girl in the Foreign Sales Department of BMS, Rider's firm. Her name's Ray Vickers. She's left there now."

"And what did she actually say?"

Jerry recognized this line of questioning about things he

remembered perfectly well as a standard technique of Feathers'. You became impatient, and then he somehow had an advantage over you. He restrained himself.

"She wasn't specific, just said there was something fishy about the way the department operated, and that it was funny Rider himself took so much interest in it. I've made a few discreet inquiries, and he does seem to have an unusual amount to do with that department."

"Don't see why you're excited."

"Not excited, sir, just interested. Since I share a flat with young Paradine—his father's an old friend of Rider's and in charge of the whole Foreign Sales Department—it seemed a good idea to keep an eye on Rider. If he's mixed up in some fiddle, you can be sure it'll be a big one."

"It sounds to me like a spiteful girl getting a bit of her own back because she's been sacked. Don't spend too much time on it, Jerry."

Jerry Maitland said blankly, "No, sir."

8

Had the whole idea of a holiday in Spain come from Amanda? Geoffrey wondered. It would be characteristic of what he knew of her to have made an arrangement by which she took the risk of sleeping with her lover while her husband was in the same house. But then what he knew of her, as he acknowledged to himself, was almost nothing. If she felt nothing but dislike for Roger, why didn't she leave him? How had she ever come to marry him? He had asked her this.

"I was an actress, and Roger was one of the backers for a play I was in. It was a terrible play, must have been the last of those 'who's for tennis?' comedies ever to have got to the West End. But then I was a terrible actress. I was a parlormaid in this, and I had to go in and say, 'Lord Hawksmoor is here, madam. I have asked him to wait in the morning room.' He was the mistress's lover, and she was receiving her *other* lover in her boudoir." She rolled her eyes.

"So what then?"

"So Roger liked the look of me. Or perhaps he fell for my South Kensington voice—all the voices in that play were South Kensington." She dropped into Cockney. "Little 'e knew that me farver 'ad a cockles-and-whelks barrow in the Old Kent."

"Are you a Cockney?"

"Course I am, ducks, a right little Cockney sparrer. Me farver kept the stall and me muvver went out charring." She changed to Old English. "And bold Sir Roger courted and wooed me. The maiden didn't take much courting—I'd had enough of theatrical lodgings. And if you're going to ask why I don't leave him, it's because I don't want to go back to them. Not ever."

He did not believe that this was the whole truth, and it had become important for him to believe that she was telling him the whole truth, but he learned nothing more. "You know about Paula, don't you? She was my wife, but Roger slept with her and then she killed herself."

"Yes, I know." The blue-green eyes that looked at him were beautiful, but empty of expression. "You must hate him."

"I don't know. He was good to me when we were children. I suppose I've always done what he wanted about most things, even taken his charity."

"Charity?"

"When he took me on at BMS, years ago now, I said to him it was blood money. If I'd been stronger-willed I'd never have taken the job. I've never been any good at it." He caught a glimpse of her face, amused and contemptuous, and was stung into saying, "You married him for money yourself, you've told me so."

"Yes, but then I'm not like you, worrying about whether you've taken blood money or not. All money's blood money. You pay in blood for what you get in cash." Her smile had the mockery of a child's sweetness. "And after you've paid, you do what you like."

So it would have been typical of her to put into Roger's head the idea of asking him. But then, after his acceptance at the end of July, he heard nothing at all from her. After a week he found himself looking at the office telephone, willing it to ring. It did so, but her voice was never at the other end of it. Perhaps she was ill? But not so ill, surely, that she could not pick up a telephone. When a fortnight had passed, the need to make contact had become so urgent that he rang the flat. There was no reply. He rang again, and she answered.

"I asked you not to ring me here."

"I wanted to know—when shall I see you?" A girl came into the office with papers. He waved her away.

"Not just at present." She might have been a housewife dismissing a hawker at the door.

"Do you mean he's found out something?"

"I didn't mention Roger."

It was humiliating, but he had to go on. "I must see you."

The faintest of sighs wafted down the telephone. "I'll ring you sometime."

Again aware of his stupidity, he had to go on. "Do you mean—"

"I mean just what I say."

"But we shall meet in Spain. You *are* coming to Spain?"

Now her voice took on a parody of upper-class languor. "To that *super* villa, yes. And my stupid stepdaughter's going to be there, and your son, who I hear is *fantastically* attractive. Darling, it's going to be such fun. Bye now."

He did not ring again. Was it necessary for him to accept that the affair was over? Could he accept it? In the following two weeks he went through an agony of spirit that he had not known since Paula's death. He considered what he liked to think of as the facts of the affair over and over again. But then what facts were there to consider? What did he know? He decided that the most likely conclusion was the most painful one, that Amanda had another lover. If she had, why was she coming to Spain? But no doubt that was something Roger would insist on.

His thoughts went round and round like a squirrel in a cage. At the chess club he lost game after game, and gave up playing Paradine's Defense. At the office his inability to grasp simple details about contracts surprised even Neasden. James, paying him a visit, played a customary game of chess with his father, and was alarmed to find himself winning. They ate a cold supper left out by Mrs. Merchant, and once or twice Geoffrey put down his knife and fork and appeared to be about to make some revelation, but in the end said nothing. When James talked about an amusing case he had attended at the Old Bailey in connection with his thesis, his father merely nibbled at a roll. He brightened only at mention of Spain.

"What's Rider's daughter like? Sheila. He said she was pretty."

"Sheila?" His father seemed barely to recognize the name. "I don't know. I've not seen her for a long time."

"I look forward to seeing her again." If he had closed his eyes he would have seen a picture of Jerry Maitland, bullet head bent, frowning over paper as he added up piquet scores. "Nice of Roger to ask me."

His father arranged knives, forks and spoons so that they formed a square. "Have you met Mrs. Rider?"

"The second wife. I don't think so. What's she like?"

His father said carefully, "Much younger than Roger. Very lively. I think you may like her."

James was fond of his father, although they had not seen much of each other since he went to university. "Is everything all right, dad?"

His father replied, quite sharply for him, "I don't know what you mean. Why do you think things are not all right, as you put it?"

"You must be pretty lonely here. You ought to get married

again." No reply to this. "You've always said the office was boring. I hope it isn't getting you down."

Geoffrey Paradine rarely made a joke, and when he did he always laughed at it himself. "My boy, the office not only got me down, it won the fight with me by a knockout years ago. I've been in a daze ever since." It was not much of a joke, but then his laugh, a kind of crow's caw, was not much of a laugh.

9

Henry Princeton arrived at Heathrow a week before Geoffrey and James Paradine flew off to Valencia. Princeton took a taxi to his hotel, after agreeing to the extortionate sum asked by the first driver he saw. They had a pleasant chat about swinging London on the way. When the time came to pay, Princeton offered a little more than half of what they had agreed.

"What the bloody hell's this?"

"Proper fare. You've got no right to ask more."

"You agreed it. Want me to call the law?"

"Why not?" said Henry Princeton amiably. "Good idea."

The driver spat. "You want to watch it, mate."

Henry Princeton's smile showed long yellow teeth. "Oh, I do watch it. I watch it all the time."

That night he saw the sights, which included a floor show at the Boy and Girl Club in Mayfair. Later he went home with one of the dancers, getting back to his hotel at 4 A.M. At nine thirty he was on the telephone to BMS, talking to Roger Rider's secretary. When the girl said that the Chairman was too busy to make an appointment, he told her that she must have got the name wrong, and that she should tell Mr. Rider that Mr. Princeton had lots of news from Australia. That afternoon Roger Rider called him. They talked for ten minutes, and when Henry Princeton put down the telephone his long yellow teeth were showing in a smile that was not pleasant. On the following morning he rang BMS again, and this time talked to the secretary of the Managing Director, Alastair Stephenson. He saw Stephenson that afternoon. The interview lasted half an hour, and, to judge from Princeton's expression when he left, it had been no more congenial to him than the telephone conversation with Rider. He spent most of that night with another of the dancers from the Boy and Girl Club. He moved in with her for five days, and spent a lot of money. Then one morning he told the surprised girl that he was going, and that afternoon took a flight for Spain.

10

"You're giving me up, then," the woman said to John Burlington Summers.

She was a big hard blonde who had seen better days but had many worse ones ahead. She had called herself a dancer and a model before she landed in Sydney's rough King's Cross. There she bought a house with the money saved while she was with her last man, let rooms in it, and called herself a landlady. She had been living with Summers for almost a year. Her name was Phyllis.

"I wouldn't say that." Summers was big too, his body thickened and his face reddened by drink. "I'll be back, Phyl. There's your guarantee. Do you think I'd leave that if I wasn't coming back?"

She looked up at the genealogical chart of the Romanovs on the wall, a confusion of complicated names, the Imperial eagle brooding above them. The faded photographs round the wall showed Grand Dukes and Grand Duchesses, some in pre-Revolutionary splendor, others driving taxis and offering menu cards, pictures taken after the fall.

"I never know whether you mean all that rubbish. Come to

that, I don't know anything about you."

"Don't call it rubbish." His bunched large fist brushed her cheek.

"I don't even know what you bloody do. Is it anything to do with that?" She jerked her thumb at the chart.

"That's my hobby. I could have been a scholar, you know that. Or you might call it my destiny. One day people are going to realize—" He left the sentence unfinished. His voice was schoolmasterly British with a hint of pomposity, at odds with his manner. He impressed and fascinated her.

"I don't even know where you're going."

"That's right."

"Or how long you'll be."

"Not more than a month. Probably less. I'll send a cable."

"You don't give a woman much chance, do you? You're a close-mouthed bastard, Johnny."

He laughed, patted her cheek again, this time with his open palm. Then he took his two shabby cases downstairs. Later she watched his cab turn the corner, looked at the chart with his name at the bottom of it, and wondered whether she would ever see him again. Men had always left her and she had never worried about it, but she would have liked to keep this one.

When John Burlington Summers booked into the Hotel Metropol at Valeta the cast was complete, the stage set for the plot against Geoffrey Paradine. A few further developments had still to occur in relation to the plot against Roger Rider.

PART TWO | The Disappearances

1

Seventy passengers step out onto the tarmac at Valencia Airport, to be received by the dry insistent heat of early afternoon. Their clothes announce them to be English; the envy with which they regard the umber faces of returning compatriots indicates that they are holiday-makers. A few are met by friends with cars, but most are package-holiday tourists, who look round anxiously on arrival. Will the tour arrangements fail, are they going to be stranded in a foreign city? But all is well. Coaches and buses sweep up bearing the names of hotels, couriers are there to make sure that the baggage is not lost. Reassured, the package tourists sink into their seats. The first hurdle has been surmounted, although many more—will they get the rooms they ordered with balcony, sea view and shower, will the hot water be hot—lie ahead.

As they get into the buses some of the girls cast regretful glances at the tall young man with long curling fair hair and sparkling blue eyes, who wears his jeans and pullover with casual elegance. Accompanied as he is, not by a girl but only by a thin small baldish man who looks gloomily at the ground, he would have been a welcome addition to any package-tour party. But as they watch a Mercedes pulls up, the driver jumps out and looks inquiringly around, the young man speaks to him, cases are collected and stowed away, the baldish man gets in the car and the young man follows him, they drive away.

"Cheer up, dad," James said as they threaded a way through Valencia's streets. "It's a holiday, you're meant to be enjoying it."

"It's a mistake, I should never have come." His son stared at him. "But perhaps everything that happens to us is predetermined, do you believe that?"

"I can't say I've thought about it much."

"Everything leads me to believe it. Otherwise why do we do things that we know to be wrong or stupid?" There seemed no reply to this. "Is suicide predetermined too? It's always the result of pressure by another human being or group of human beings that becomes intolerable."

"I don't think that has anything to do with things being predetermined. Rather the contrary, I should say. It seems to imply free will. If you can resist the pressure—"

Geoffrey was not really interested in the argument, only in his reflections. "Your mother committed suicide. I was partly responsible for her death. I've never told you."

James rather prided himself on his capacity for self-analysis. He wondered what he felt about this, and decided that he felt nothing. Why should he? He barely remembered his mother. Looking sideways at his father's tight, agonized little face, however, he felt sympathy.

"Dad, I don't mind about it. After all, it was between the two of you, and it was a long time ago. And I don't see why you should be predestined to talk about it at this particular place and time."

"Rider was responsible too, that's why I'm thinking about it. I shouldn't have come here. It was stupid. And wrong."

James wondered whether he should ask anything more about his mother's death, and decided against it. "Rodríguez speaks English," he said by way of warning to his father not to say anything further about Rider. "Isn't that so, Rodríguez?"

The thickish neck in front of them did not move. "Sí, I have been a little while in England. I learn there."

"How far is it to Valeta?"

"Fifty-five kilometers, perhaps sixty."

"Is Mr. Rider there yet?"

"He is not arriving yet." Rodríguez's accent was strong, but his comprehension obviously good. Now he turned, revealing a beetling brow, a broken nose, a prognathous jaw. Not a prepossessing face, James thought; Lombroso would immediately have classified him as a criminal type. "I 'ave on the radio, all right?" he asked.

James looked at his father, who seemed not to have heard. "Of course."

The sound that filled the car was recognizably that of a commentator at a football match. Listening more closely, James was surprised to hear familiar names. "Surely that's Chelsea?"

"Sí. Chelsea and Real Madrid. You follow the futbol?"

"I watch Chelsea, yes. And play a bit myself."

A roar of sound came from the set. Rodríguez let go of the wheel, the car moved alarmingly across the road. An oncoming car blasted furiously at them. The commentator's hysterical voice rose above the hysteria of the crowd. Chelsea had scored.

Rodríguez regained control. "Hosgood hisgood," he said.

"What's that?"

"It is what they shout in Chelsea, hosgood hisgood."

"Osgood is good—yes, I see. They don't shout it as much as they used to do, he's getting on a bit."

" 'E's scored."

They continued with a brisk discussion of the merits of various English clubs, and a comparison of English and Spanish football. His father, who had been completely silent, murmured something and then repeated it.

"What I was saying. Don't take too much notice of it."

"You mean it's not true?"

"I'll tell you about it one day. I'm glad you were able to come."

What do I think of in relation to *mother?* James wondered. A sort of presence bending over me, a smell of cologne, early bedtime stories. He could get no further than that, but he had no sense of deprivation. "Dad, why did you never marry again?"

"Your mother and I were happy." He lingered on the word. "And I wanted to bring you up myself. Though I didn't do that in the end. I sent you to boarding school after Rider gave me the job. You might say it was his doing. I saw very little of you."

He sounded so miserable that James laughed. "Never mind, it didn't turn out that badly. And we're seeing each other now."

Geoffrey Paradine gripped his son's hand, then released it.

2

"Doesn't this beat flying?" Roger kept asking. He enumerated the advantages as they drove through France. You saw the country, you talked to people (although not with great effect, since many of them failed to understand Roger's pidgin French), you ate marvelous meals instead of the plastic muck on the plane. Amanda showed her boredom with all this, but Sheila had always found her father's enthusiasm enjoyable in small doses. And besides, what he said about the food was true. Her memory lingered over quenelles of trout, a particular plate of crudités.

They were making good time when they crossed the Spanish border, but then Roger insisted on taking an attractive-looking minor road and they found themselves on the way to Lérida instead of to Barcelona. Roger was not disturbed. He drove the Bentley with supreme confidence, although not with particular skill, and as he drove he opened his mouth and bellowed:

"I'm a happy man, a very strange thing for a man in my *po-si-ti-on*,
But I'm a hap-hap-happy man, I have a happy *dis-po-si-ti-on.*"

His wife sat beside him, his daughter in the back. Amanda said languidly, "Not tuneful, but noisy."

He changed tune and lyric:

> "Said the girlie to the boysie
> Must you be so noisy?
> Said the boy to his inamorata
> Just let me past your garter.

I could go on like that for hours."

"You don't surprise me."

In the back Sheila sighed. There was no doubt that Roger could be very trying.

He turned left. "Just another fifteen miles and we should be back on the motorway somewhere the right side of Tarragona. After that it's about a hundred and fifty kilometers. Two hours and a half. Less. We shall be late, but María will have saved something."

"You should have told her in advance that we might be late," Amanda said.

He puffed out his chest and bawled, operatic style:

> "I could not speak, the line was out of o-o-order,
> But if your wish, oh, if your wish is food,
> Then we will find a restaurant or a ca-a-afé,
> And there we'll dine to suit the passing mood.

I'm really in form, wouldn't you say?"

"Most of these little Spanish places are awful. Unknown fish cooked in rancid oil." Amanda shivered delicately.

"To stop or not to stop, that is the question."

"If you hadn't taken what was obviously the wrong road, it's a question that would never have arisen."

"Aren't you enjoying this drive? You have no soul, woman."

Sheila wondered if her father's patience would break. She knew him as a patient man who just occasionally gave way to fits of violent anger. On the rare occasions when she had seen these, they frightened her. Was there a hint of thunder in his voice as he asked now, "You like the villa, don't you?"

"It's a villa by the sea. What more can you say?"

Sheila thought how much she disliked her stepmother.

"You mean it might as well be at Skegness or Southport. If that's all you can say, you *are* soulless. No imagination."

"Only businessmen have imagination, I realize that."

The dusk had faded to darkness. Roger switched on his headlights, and as if at a signal the engine suddenly died. The car came gently to a standstill. He tried the starter half a dozen times without effect, got out with a torch, opened the bonnet and looked speculatively inside. He came back and tapped the fuel gauge, which had been reading just under a half. It dropped instantly to zero.

"No petrol."

"That's all it needed." As though she could no longer bear to be inside the vehicle, Amanda opened the door and walked up and down the verge of the road.

"You're sure?" Sheila got out too. They had stopped beside an olive grove. She found a straight thin piece of wood and pushed it into the tank. It came out practically dry. Sheila knew that Amanda was angry when an edge of feeling entered her usually calm voice.

"If you had any sense, you'd have realized from the distance we'd gone since you last filled up that the petrol gauge was wrong."

"Shut up, you're not helping. Get back in the car." Amanda, surprisingly, got back into the car.

The Natural Man of Sheila's imagination would speak with total candor, ignoring the conventional civilities practiced by most people. She felt that her father approached the Natural Man on the few occasions when she had heard him thunder, and she expected that the storm would break now, but he said nothing more. Instead he examined their map of Spain under the headlight, which showed his broad red face, blunt undistinguished features, with something bull-like about the whole head. She leaned over his shoulder. There was a delicious scent in the air. The map showed that they were on a side road between Lérida and Tarragona, which they knew already, that the nearest village was named Hilar, and that it might be anything from one to three miles ahead.

He straightened up, not so much the Natural Man as the Captain of Industry. "Right. Sheila, I suggest we set out to walk to this place Hilar. Amanda, you stay here, try to stop a passing motorist if there is one, and get some petrol. If you have any luck, drive down and pick us up. Agreed?"

"You can do what you like," Amanda said. "But if you think I'm going to stand in the road waving cars down, you're quite wrong."

"I didn't suggest that. Just try listening to what I say."

"I shall shut myself in until you come back. If somebody happens to stop, all right. But nobody will, I can tell you that."

"Sheila can stay here and try to flag down a car."

"Oh, no, take her by all means. I know you like a little feminine admiration."

He leaned into the car, caught her wrist, and twisted it. Sheila felt a small thrill of pleasure. The Natural Man was at work. But all he said was "Don't push it, Amanda. One day you'll go too far."

She replied with an affected languor which Sheila had heard before, and which sounded to her ridiculous. "Darling, if I'm so mad keen to get there, it's because I do so long to see you and your old friend Geoffrey together. And would you let go of my wrist? You're hurting."

He let go. "What the hell are you talking about?"

"Darling, you know you've got a *thing* about Geoffrey. I mean, you know you love being his oldest friend *and* his boss, isn't that so? I mean, you can show all the time that you're the boss, and he has to say, oh, isn't it super, I *love* to have my face trodden on. And then you tread on it. Really, that's such fun."

Sheila thought now, now the storm will break, perhaps he'll hit her. Her father seemed about to do that. Then he started off down the road without warning, so that Sheila had to run a step or two to catch up with him. When they were out of range of the headlights, darkness was absolute, except for the torch illuminating a few yards of metaled road ahead. She breathed in deeply.

"You know, I love things like this—the car breaking down and being stranded. I hate to depend so much on machinery, almost as if it controlled us. This is romantic. I believe I could live in a place like this."

"Could you, now? Would you say my life was? Romantic, I mean."

"Oh, no," she said decisively. He laughed. She relented slightly. "Captain of Industry, you mean—all that stuff. I suppose some people would call it romantic."

"Rags to riches, Malbite Street to Pevering Manor, you don't think that's romantic at all? Do you remember Malbite Street?"

"I remember going there for Christmas sometimes. I didn't like it, used to wonder why we went."

"Geoffrey and I grew up there together, you know that. Only he's never moved on."

"There's no need to use that tone. You just have more money than him, that's all."

"You think so? Then I daresay you believe those things Amanda was saying."

"I don't know anything about that. I don't remember him much."

They turned a bend in the road. A car approached and they waved, but it ignored them. Sheila thought about Amanda sitting in the Bentley. "Why did you marry her?"

"You've got to have somebody to sit at the end of a table, talk to people, look ornamental."

"*Got* to? A lot of people manage without."

"Not people in my position."

"God, daddy, you can be pompous. I do think she's a ghastly woman."

When the hearty facetiousness had gone from his voice it sounded heavy as plum pudding. "Would it be any answer to say that I was crazy about her?"

"I see you're using the past tense."

"You're a sharp girl." His booming laugh sounded odd in the empty space. "But it's past and present tense. There's something quite special about her."

"I don't see it."

"I daresay you don't. But it still exists."

"You must realize she's out for what she can get."

"We all are. In one way or another. That's something you learn."

"A businessman's philosophy."

"I daresay," he said again. "It's true, though. Sometimes you have to do things you don't like—you learn that too. You make mistakes and they find you out. Then you have to do something about them."

"Amanda, you mean? I should certainly call her one of your mistakes."

"You've got spirit. I like that. Most people haven't. What Amanda said back there was true. People lie down and ask you to step on them, so what else can you do? It's almost a duty."

"I call that fascism."

"Just a word. Calling a name. I didn't know you disapproved so much of your old dad." He put a hand on her shoulder in the dark. "Remember, girl, it was you who cut yourself off from me, not the other way round. It's your own doing that you're teaching art to snotty little kids who couldn't care less if every painting in the world was destroyed next week."

"I'll remember."

The hand was removed. "If anything happens to me, though, you'll be all right." Something about the tone had an ominous sound.

"What do you mean?"

"Just what I say. Remember it."

It took them twenty minutes to reach Hilar, and then there was no petrol station in the village. When they returned empty-handed to the car, Amanda was asleep on the back seat, covered by a rug. She stayed where she was. Roger and Sheila slept in the front, or tried to. At seven in the morning a German tourist stopped, and gave them a gallon of petrol from the can that, as he told them with pride, he always carried.

Afterward, Sheila saw with surprise, her father was his usual self, making bad jokes, rubbing the bristles on his chin and asking if the sound made them shiver, hee-hawing like a donkey when they approached a restaurant, to show that he was hungry. The somber man who had talked to her on the road at night had vanished. They reached the villa at ten thirty, and Amanda went straight to bed.

3

When the Riders arrived, James was finishing a letter.

James Paradine, student in the bloody fields of criminal literature, at present in the Villa Victoria, Valeta, to his friend Jeremy Maitland, toiler and moiler among villains on that patch known as the Metropolitan Police area. Greetings.

We have arrived. I have dived, swimmer into cleanness leaping (Rupert Brooke, poet, you ignorant sod) into the pool, I look out from the picture window of my bedroom onto green lawn and beyond it blue blue sea. Cicadas sound, dragonflies dart, there is the endless susurrus of the sea. (Just look up anything you don't know in the dictionary.) It's perfect. Almost. Wish you were here.

But since you're not, let me begin by one of those exercises in observation which are essential to anybody concerned with crime. The Villa Victoria, as you might expect, is pretty splendid. It's one of three at the end of the village, and they form a self-contained little enclave on a promontory sticking out into the sea. Half a mile away the tower blocks of holiday flats and the slab-faced hotels begin, but we are separate, a thing apart. The three villas date back to around 1900, I suppose, and the style is your period Spanish-Moorish with a touch of your Greco-Roman, or that's how it seems to me. And all brought up to date and modernized, with picture windows, etc. In outrageous bad taste, I'm sure, but frankly I love it. Each villa different, each with its own garden separated from the next by a lot of iron fretwork, and then a steep descent by steps into the sea. Tennis court, table tennis, and in a place on the beach motorboat, speedboat, water-skiing equipment, etc. Up above again big rooms, elegant in an old-fashioned way, but all modernized.

So that's the setting. What about the jewel that should shine within it, the genius and genial host, our Roger? So far he hasn't arrived. He was due last night, plus wife and allegedly pretty daughter, and there's been no word, but actually this isn't so surprising because our phone is out of order. Probably they've done it leisurely and stopped an extra night on the way. So I can't at the moment let you have a picture of the Great Man unbuttoned among friends, or tell you what he's doing and planning.

I suspect though that, whatever it is you're looking for, you're going to be disappointed by anything personal I send you, because as I remember Our Roger (of course I've seen him very little since I was a child), he's a pretty fair bore.

But don't be afraid, old cock. When he turns up I will observe, note and faithfully report. It would have helped if you could have given me some idea of what I'm supposed to be reporting *on*, but I'll do my best.

Back to facts. The villa is looked after by Rodríguez and María. She cooks, he waits, drives the car and seems to be a general handyman. She is slightly mustached, he looks distinctly villainous but has a passion for soccer, so he can't be all bad. There are a few other staff dotted about, but the place is comfortable rather than luxurious. Nothing else in particular strikes me about it, but, as I say, I don't know what you want to know. Nothing at all, very likely.

Wish you were here, as I say. Send a line and tell me the news. If you're planning an orgy, kindly have some regard for my sheets. Haven't found any local talent myself. Played chess last night with me da, who's in a *very* odd mood.

More later.

Yours ever,
James

P.S. They have arrived! As I finished this letter. Gave a stylish wave from my balcony to Mrs. R (looking furious, went straight to bed), Sheila (only saw her for a moment, waved back) and RR. Seems they ran out of petrol and spent the night in the car. RR's greeting at sight of me was "My, you're much taller. And you've certainly filled out." A Golden Treasury of RR sayings in my next.

4

In his thesis James planned to develop the idea that the United States was the country in which real and fictional crime had interlocked most completely. It was the country in which the activities of gangsters seemed most like fiction (those Chicago gangster funerals of the Twenties, the Mafia wars later on), and also in which the crime fiction, like that of Hammett and Chandler, seemed most real. And if it was true that real-life criminals picked up the use of the word "gunsel" from Dashiell Hammett, wasn't that an instance of the Oscarian theory that life imitates art? He had brought out a number of books on American crime, and was sitting on the lawn reading *20,000 Years in Sing Sing* when a voice said, "Cousin James."

He removed his dark glasses, got to his feet and had his first close view of Sheila Rider. It was obvious at once that she was not what he would have chosen as a cure for incipient homosexuality. There was nothing wrong with her round innocent features, except that he liked straight-nosed classical women, and nothing wrong with her figure except that it curved about like that of an Edwardian Gaiety Girl and he preferred women to be thin as rails. The truly distressing thing about her, though, was the clothes she wore. She had on a purplish smock which had across it thick diagonal stripes in a sort of dingy gold. The smock also, remarkably, was tight rather than loose, so that she might have been slightly pregnant. The sketchbook she carried seemed a poor excuse for such a garment.

"And Cousin Sheila," he said. "We haven't met for years."

During the commonplaces that followed, about the beauty of

the villa and the sea, Sheila assessed James. She was susceptible to masculine good looks, and it was impossible not to be aware of his extreme handsomeness. That curling golden hair, the well-shaped nose and long elegant hands—he looked not so much like a film star (film stars didn't now, and perhaps never had, looked like that) as like some unfashionably beautiful poet. He certainly didn't resemble the Natural Man of her imagination, and he seemed prepared to go on with this boring conversation forever. She saw no reason why she should not put an end to it.

"Let's stop talking this nonsense, then you can get on with your reading and I can try to catch a bit of this." She opened the sketchbook.

He was amused. "Is it rubbish?"

She made pencil strokes while she spoke. "Everything that doesn't reflect real feeling is rubbish, a sort of conventional sign language that's strictly meaningless."

He was amused again. Perhaps she would look better in something other than that frightful smock? "I should have thought the essence of sign language was that it conveyed some meaning."

"Word-spinning. What do you do?" He told her. "And when you've got your Ph.D., what then? Join the army of teachers, like me? That's a fairly useless occupation."

He abandoned *Sing Sing*. "If you think it's useless, why not do something else?"

"What else?" She did not look at him, but continued sketching, changing from one pencil to another, holding the first between her teeth. He was reminded for a moment of Jerry. "I've got a rich father, he'd have paid for me at an art school, liked nothing better, but all you learn at art school is how to keep in step with tomorrow's fashion. If you've got anything in you, you make it alone, okay? I tried that, but I don't have anything. I know what to do, but I can't do it. So I teach. A fairly useless occupation, as I say, but not quite. Once a year there's a boy or girl who has something genuine and sees things freshly. Naturally. Not like this."

He looked at what she had done. She had sketched a corner of the garden, bristling cacti, sword-bladed bushes, open-petaled flowers like gaping throats. But she was right, the drawing had the discretion and gentility absent from her conversation; the hostile murderous flowers and plants looked gentle as roses. He said that he was going to swim. She changed into an unsuitable flowered bikini, and came in with him. He swam, as he did everything, with elegance, but she reached the raft first. As they stretched out on it he asked if she wanted to go in to the village later, and she agreed without too much enthusiasm.

James thought her at least an unusual girl, and wished that she looked a bit different. Sheila, lying beside him, was very conscious of his body. She thought him one of the most beautiful young men she had ever seen, and sexually attractive too, which was not quite the same thing. The Natural Woman would no doubt express her feelings by putting a hand on his body, but she could not bring herself to do that. They had been lying there a quarter of an hour when Roger hailed them from the lawn.

"Drinks on the terraza," he called.

"Terraza indeed," Sheila said as they swam back. "Why the hell doesn't he call it a terrace?"

Roger hands round drinks in a hostly manner. "Cuba libres. Watch out for them, they may seem innocuous but they do pack a sting. Well, how do you like it? I don't mean the drink, the place. Quite something, isn't it, eh, Geoff?"

Geoffrey wears shorts that are not quite short enough, a tasteful flowered shirt. His arms and legs look like white sticks. A pocket chessboard is beside him, and he does not look up from it. "Very nice."

"That's our Geoff, master of understatement."

Amanda is wearing a plain sleeveless dark-blue dress that makes her look no older than her stepdaughter. She takes one sip of her cuba libre, pushes it aside. "Can I have a Campari and soda?"

Roger pours the drink, takes it over, says mildly enough, "You used to say there was nothing you liked more than a cuba libre."

"My taste has changed. Tastes do change, you know." •

Roger appears about to reply to this, but doesn't. Geoffrey looks up from his chess set, then down again. James feels that the atmosphere is one you could cut with a knife. The Riders are obviously on bad terms, but why does his father seem so tense?

Amanda goes on talking. "Are we going to be on our own here for a whole month? Did you warn them that there's really nothing to do?"

"The Mattinglys are coming out at the end of next week. And later on Bill Parr and his latest girl friend."

"Perhaps we can amuse ourselves until then." Her look flicks rapidly between Roger, Geoffrey and James, as though wondering which of them is most likely to be amusing. A ridiculous act, James thinks, but quite impressive in its way.

Roger went on as though she had not spoken. "Just for a few days I want to get some peace. My idea of a holiday is just sitting around on a beach, splashing about in the sea, soaking up sun, doing nothing. God knows I never get any peace at the office. That's why I didn't bring a secretary out. People say how d'you manage without one, I say I'd never get a decent holiday *with* one. Bring a secretary and you can be sure there'll be papers to sign, urgent messages and all that."

"But surely they know where you are," James said.

"Certainly they do, but they won't bother me. Miss Battleaxe —that's the name I give to my secretary—Miss Battleaxe makes sure nothing gets through except what's really important. You'd be surprised how little that is, how much people find they can do on their own if they have to." He drained his glass, looked at Geoff. "Most people won't take chances. That's why I've got where I am, never afraid to take chances."

Sheila clapped her hands ironically. Roger addressed James, who had been thinking that a month of this would be more than he could stand.

"What are you doing, eh, my lad?" When he had been told, he

said, "Waste of time, if I may be blunt."

"Sheila's just told me much the same."

"She's a bright girl. Look at it this way. By the time you've got your degree, looked around and made a couple of false starts, you'll be almost ready for your old-age pension." He tapped his forehead. "I never had too much up there, not a quarter as much as your father. But I could sell things. So I went out and sold them, and got on with it. Had my failures, but I've always been able to find a way round things. If you can't do something one way, try another, and don't be afraid of taking chances. That's my advice."

James said he would remember. Then he heard Amanda's drawl.

"Darling, you needn't go on like that. He's not a reporter. Nobody's taking it down."

Roger's shoulders jerked, as though he had been stung by a wasp. At the same moment Rodríguez appeared at the end of the terrace. He was wearing a white jacket and trousers, which increased the villainous nature of his appearance. "Luncheon is served."

Lunch was delicious, a Spanish omelet followed by veal in a cream sauce. With it they drank a local wine with a nutty, almost gritty flavor. Dinner the previous evening had been a magnificent paella. Perhaps, James thought, he should send Jerry a list of meals eaten and drink consumed? While they were eating the omelet, Roger was called to the telephone. Amanda raised her brows when he returned.

"That was the office. Alastair." James expected Amanda to say something about his boast of being left alone during a holiday, but she remained silent. Roger pushed the rest of his omelet aside, and looked from James to Sheila.

"Did I hear you say you were going in to Valeta? I want to go myself—the car's pulling over to one side. Like a lift? It's quite a walk into the village."

They accepted the lift. It occurred to James that driving in to the village was hardly soaking up sun and doing nothing.

The garage recommended by Rodríguez was on the outskirts of Valeta. They left Roger there trying to tell the garage man what was wrong, with the help of a Spanish phrase book. James wondered why Rodríguez couldn't have taken in the car, and decided that in spite of what he had said, Roger was probably the kind of man who insisted on doing things himself.

There was not much to see in Valeta. The village remained barely touched by the prosperity that had come with the slab-sided hotels. They walked down the long dusty street, where some of the shops had closed because the tourist season was near its end. The rest, which had reopened after the siesta, sold crude pottery, sword paper-knives with *Toledo* stamped on the blade, postcards showing bullfights and dishes of paella. Sheila had changed into a sleeveless acid-lemon shirt, bright-green trousers tight round the buttocks, and sandals in a different shade of yellow.

"Don't you like them?" They were in a shop looking at some pottery.

"Like what?"

"My sandals. You keep staring at them."

"Not much, no."

"What's wrong with them?"

"I think I'd like them better if they were in a neutral color." He thought of saying that for an art teacher she was markedly deficient in color sense, but refrained. They went into a small museum which showed all, and more than, anybody could have wished to know about wine-making in the region, decided that they had exhausted the attractions of Valeta, and started the walk back. As they neared the end of the main street James thought that he saw Rider's bulky figure turn the corner ahead. He was talking to another man of about the same height. When they reached the corner there was no sign of him, and James concluded that perhaps he had been mistaken. Or perhaps the man had something to do with the garage.

They left the road, walked back along the beach. The sun was hot. Sheila took off her sandals and carried them. A little more than halfway back they lay down, exhausted, in a patch of shade offered by rocks. James was conscious of Sheila's bare arms. Would it be unfair to call them brawny? No doubt it would. They were certainly less sizable than Jerry's, so why was the image that came to his mind one of inflated bicycle tubes? He closed his eyes and saw patterns of red behind the lids. She said something that he did not hear.

"What's that?"

She was lying on her stomach looking at him. "Oh, Christ. What I said was, you turn me on. Physically, I mean—I don't know that I like you much otherwise. How do *you* feel?"

"Are you always this direct?"

"What's the point in being anything else? But I have the idea you can't bear the sight of me. If so, I might as well know it."

He considered this judicially. "I don't much like your taste in clothes. And perhaps you could do with losing a bit of weight."

Her eyes glowed with what might have been amusement or anger. She had rather fine eyes. "Anything else?"

Why shouldn't his candor equal hers? "I share a flat with a friend in London. A man, I mean."

"*Oh.*" She leaned on one elbow, stared at him with interest. "You mean you're queer? I can see you'd be attractive to men, but somehow it never struck me you'd be queer. Do you find women repulsive?"

"I—"

"Because of course I can understand that. The thing is, though, I must say I should have thought it was generally rather unsatisfactory. I mean, what do you actually *do?*"

"You're a remarkable girl."

"Because I want to know, you mean? Well, of course, I do know in a way, you don't have to spell it out. I had some lesbian experiences, I suppose you'd call them, at school. But what I really mean is, with queers one's the man and the other's the woman, isn't that right? If you're the man, then there might be some hope for me. But if you're the woman—well."

"It's not usually that simple. At the moment we don't do anything."

"Really?" She chewed a fingernail, waiting for him to go on.

"I'm pretty sure he's straight—you know, heterosexual. I've never made any approach."

"I think you should," she said decidedly. "Get it settled one way or the other. I mean, it must be very unsatisfactory."

"I suppose so. Though it's also true that—I mean, I've slept with girls. And had homosexual experiences too, though not all that many. The thing is, you see, I'm not sure."

"And what you like best is slim boyish girls, I suppose. What about my stepmother? You find her attractive? She's a bitch."

"I daresay. I do think she's attractive."

"It's a slimming campaign for me, I see that." She jumped up, began to do exercises, then laughed. "Don't worry. You're safe, I don't think I can slim. It's a pity, though."

James agreed that it was a pity. They walked the rest of the way back to the villa.

Geoffrey Paradine sat on the terrace in the shade under an awning, replaying one of the Spassky-Fischer games in the world championship. Fischer had played a Sicilian Defense, and it seemed to Geoffrey that if he had used the Paradine Defense he would have improved his position in the middle game. But it was necessary to envisage Spassky's responses, and this he found himself quite unable to do in his state of tension. He put away the chess set, walked across the lawn and stared at the sea twenty feet below. Here in the sun it was very hot. The water gleamed like blue steel. He turned to face the villa, looked up at the first floor. The shutters of the room at the end were drawn. Amanda was there. She had hardly spoken a word to him since her arrival.

He walked back to the house, stood inside the living room, then went to the kitchen quarters. There was nobody about. Rodríguez and María were no doubt having their siesta. He went up the marble interior stairs, then paused. The need to talk to Amanda fretted him like a rash. He walked down the passage, pushed open the end door.

For a moment he could see nothing. He went in and closed the door, stumbling a little. Her voice, cool as ice water, said, "Yes?"

The click of a light switch and she was visible, lying under a sheet. "What are you doing in here?" All he could do was stare at her and stammer out her name. She looked at her watch. "If Roger comes back and finds you in our room, he won't be pleased."

"I've got to talk to you."

"Must you? Perhaps you'd open the shutters." He did so. She murmured, "Yes?"

"You said you were longing to be out here, that we should—have fun." His voice trailed away. He was aware of the incongruity of this, a man of his age talking about having fun.

"I don't think so. I said it would be fun out here, and that it was a super villa. It is super, don't you think?"

"You know very well—"

"I know I didn't say anything about *us* having fun. I do like the look of your James, I must say. He's quite fantastically attractive."

"You mean it's over, we're finished. Is that what you mean? You can't do that." He was ashamed of the words even as they poured from him, ashamed of the miserable begging tone.

"Come and sit. Here." She patted the bed. Obediently he went and sat on it. "Now, let's be clear about this. I made no promises to you. I can do anything I like, so can you. Agreed?" He nodded. "Good. Now, at present the answer is no. I'm not in the mood. Tomorrow it may be yes. Do you understand?"

He said, appalled, "But you can't behave like that. You mustn't."

"Oh, really?" she said with assumed languor, then burst out laughing. "If you could see yourself. Those white legs and knobbly knees."

Suddenly it was all too much, the nearness of her body, the almost open mockery of her manner, the feeling that he had been deceived and used. He leaned over, gripped her shoulders and pulled away the sheet and there she was, naked and slippery as a fish, twisting away from him and still laughing. He brought his hands up to her neck to stop the laughter, but she still slithered away, her neck itself seeming slippery. He clung on to it, pleased to see the laugh wiped out and a look of fear take its place, pleased also to find an unsuspected strength in his hands so that they were impervious to all the attempts of her own hands to displace them, glad above all to be teaching her a lesson. Then she brought up her knee sharply to his genitals, and although her legs were still under the sheet the impact was painful. He let go.

"You tried to strangle me." She jumped out of bed, sobbing for breath, and went over to the glass, her hands touching her neck.

"I'm sorry. I didn't mean— It was the way you talked."

"Get out." The languor had gone, and there was no doubt now about her Cockney origin. The words sounded like *git aht*.

"Amanda, please."

"I said bloody well *git aht*."

He was outside the door when he heard feet on the stairs. It was Roger, staring at him in a surprise that was perfectly natural, for this end of the passage led only to the bedroom on the one side and the bathroom on the other. Geoffrey muttered something unintelligible even to himself, and went past. Roger looked thoughtfully after him before entering the bedroom.

Five thirty. James stood looking through binoculars at the speedboat arched high above the waves, trailed by a faint line of spittle. The two figures in it were recognizable, his father gripping the side of the boat, Roger at the wheel. Roger had relinquished the ridiculous yachting cap he had worn when they started out. They were both wearing life jackets. As he watched, the boat turned sharply, tilted, straightened up again. Why did he have this feeling that something unpleasant was about to happen? He put down the binoculars, as though relinquishing them might help to cancel out whatever danger might exist, and saw that Rodríguez stood near him, also watching. The speedboat rounded a buoy out in the bay, and turned again in a swirl of foam.

"That was a sharp turn. But I expect Señor Rider is good with the boat."

Rodríguez shrugged. "I don't know. I am only here this year."

"But you know how to handle the speedboat. I saw you out with it this morning."

"That's right, I use the boat. I can do anything." He smiled, showing a couple of blackened teeth, then put his hands together almost at right angles. "I think he go too much like this, eh?"

"That's just Roger having fun. He knows what he's doing." Amanda had come out. She picked up the glasses and looked through them briefly. "He's having a wonderful time, giving your father a fright. He's still very schoolboyish, you know. I hope your father doesn't mind."

"I don't suppose so. After all, they were schoolboys together."

"So they were. I'm going to the Bar Central down the road for a drink. Like to come?"

It would have been difficult to say no, and in any case he was not inclined to. As they went out of the garden and down the road she talked, as it seemed, easily and unaffectedly, yet dropping at times from one accent to another, so that she gave the impression of playing a part.

"Very lush and comfortable back there, why don't we just sit out and have a drink brought by our broken-nosed chum, you may ask? Or wait for Roger to come back and play mine host? Somehow it's a bit stifling, don't you find that? I don't suppose you do, it's your first visit and you've only been here a day. But meself, I like to sit in a little caff and watch the world go by. And here it is. You can buy me a vermouth."

The Bar Central stood a little back from the road, with iron tables and chairs. He ordered two vermouths. Amanda looked out at the road as she spoke to him, her profile boyish and delicate. Her tone was conversational, yet it produced upon him the feeling of artifice.

"Your father tried to rape me this afternoon."

He wondered whether he had heard this correctly, decided that he had, and decided also to reply in her own offhand manner. "How tiresome. Or was it enjoyable?"

"You don't believe me?" She took off the silk scarf round her neck. There were red marks that might have been made by fingers. "He tried to strangle me too. Part of it, you might say. I gave him a kick where it did most good."

"You're making this up," he said, though he was slightly shaken. "I can't imagine dad trying to rape anyone. And anyway, you know what the police say—any woman who claims she's been raped by just one man was at least partly consenting."

"That must be nice to know when it's happened." In the same conversational tone she said, "You'd better know this: I've been having an affair with Geoffrey. It's finished, but he wants it to go on. That's why he came to my room this afternoon, and why this happened." She touched her neck.

It is often difficult to see one's parents in anything but a parental role, yet James's reaction was not one of disbelief but of distress. He was surprised to find himself upset by what she had said, more surprised to realize that the feeling sprang from a deep affection for his father which he had not known to exist.

"What can I do about it?"

"If Roger gets to know, there'll be trouble. He must have seen Geoffrey leaving this afternoon."

"What sort of trouble?"

"Roger might do something to Geoffrey. Or, the way he's feeling, Geoffrey might do something to Roger. They've got a funny relationship, those two."

"I don't see what I can do."

"Talk to your father, persuade him to go home." She said with the utmost calmness, "I'm worried about what may happen."

He remembered that odd conversation in the car on the way to the villa. He remembered Rodríguez's hands at right angles: *I think he go too much like this, eh?*

A Volkswagen braked with a flurry of dust to avoid a man crossing the road. The man, whose panama hat had fallen off, cursed the driver in English. The driver leaned out and cursed back in German, and the man in the road changed to fluent German. The Volkswagen drove away. The man sat down at one of the tables, ordered a Fundador, stared at them. When the drink came he lifted it in the air and proposed a toast. "Anastasia."

Roger cut the engine. Noise died. They floated placidly.

"Handles beautifully, doesn't she? What's up, Geoff? You're shivering."

"I'm wet." Geoffrey took off the bulky life jacket.

"Oh, a life on the ocean wave, that's the life for a jolly Jack Tar," Roger caroled. "But you were never too keen on the watery element, were you? Remember on that school outing to Brighton when Brownie Barnes held you under, and I had to butt him in the stomach to get you away? Don't suppose you've ever liked the briny too much since then. Me, I love it. I'm not much for poetry, you know that, but I know that poem of Masefield's about going down to the sea again by heart. I'm a little damp too, come to think of it." He took off his own life jacket. They both wore swimming trunks.

There was a breeze, and in spite of the hot sun Geoffrey felt it on the white chicken flesh of his body. "You wanted to talk to me about something."

The sun was turning Roger's ruddy face a brickish color. The water lapped gently at the boat; the land looked very far away. "Is anything worrying you, Geoff? Anything you'd like to tell me?" Geoffrey shook his head. "What do you think about the department?"

"The department?"

"It doesn't seem to me it's running as it should. I feel you may have got a bit stale, need a change. What d'you say?"

"And that's what you wanted to talk about?"

"What else? I thought perhaps one of the home departments, say Home Retail Division. How would you fancy that? Old Davidson there is due to be put out to pasture. Then we might promote Neasden, who seems a bright lad."

"You know I don't mind. I mean, I never really understood all the workings of the department anyway. If it hadn't been for you I should never have kept the job, you know that."

"Helped you all along the line, haven't I? And you've repaid it. Faithful service to BMS and all that. And friendship to me. Only not quite so much lately."

There was water in the bottom of the boat, and Roger had moved down from the bow and was scooping it out with a tin.

The sun had been obscured for a few moments. Geoffrey found himself shivering. "I don't understand."

"Not getting back from lunch till four o'clock or later. That won't do. It's got to end, Geoff. I can't have that. Agreed?"

He put down the can. His body, large and powerful, was only a yard away from his friend's. Geoffrey was aware, as he had been in childhood, of his own puny physical structure. His feelings then when Roger protected him had always been a blend of relief and fear. Now Roger stood up and his body appeared gigantic, a statue blocking out the returning sun. The great blunt head looked downward at Geoffrey, and he knew fear. Then Roger was at the other end of the boat, smiling.

"Better time-keeping, eh, Geoff? A bit less time spent at the old chess club. Otherwise—"

He started the engine, and any other words were lost in the noise.

"Anastasia's granddaughter," the man said. He was big, perhaps in his middle fifties. He wore a pair of blue denim trousers, a khaki shirt and sandals. His features were flat and rather brutish, his small eyes a boiled blue.

"Were you speaking to me?" James recognized this pseudo-aristocratic hauteur as one of Amanda's conversational styles.

The man got up, brought his chair across to them, sat. "There's no doubt about it. The bone structure is unmistakable. I could show you a dozen photographs."

"I don't know what you're talking about."

He felt in his pockets, produced tobacco and a machine, rolled a cigarette. "I've given the last fifteen years of my life to tracing the descendants of the Grand Duchess Anastasia."

"The one who was involved in that court case?" James asked.

"Ah, well now, whether *she* was Anastasia is very doubtful, very doubtful indeed. The point is this. The Russian royals were supposed to have been killed at Ekaterinburg in 1918, and perhaps some of them were. There's very little real evidence either way. But what there's no doubt of at all is that Anastasia survived. I've got a dossier about her escape and her descendants that covers twelve countries."

James looked at Amanda. "Do you know of any Russian ancestors?" Amanda shook her head. She was looking at the man with an expression combining wariness and annoyance. "What are you going to do with your dossier?"

There was a pop. The long-haired boy who served drinks was pouring champagne. The man raised one of them. "To one of Anastasia's most beautiful descendants. It should be Georgian champagne, not Spanish. A desecration, I'm afraid."

"I don't care for Spanish champagne." Amanda pushed her glass aside. James recognized the technique she had used with the cuba libre, but the man appeared not to hear her. He spoke to James.

"What purpose? A good question. Two reasons. I am myself the grandson of the Grand Duke Dimitri, who was banned from court for his part in the murder of Rasputin. My father was Count Nicholas Michailovitch Dashkov. The Grand Duke never publicly acknowledged his paternity, but I am myself entitled to the appellation of Count, though I never use it."

James resisted the temptation to laugh. The man's expression made him realize this would not be wise.

"I will tell you something else. The male members of the line are psychic. I knew when I walked up here that something interesting would happen. And something else, too: Anastasia's descendants are unlucky. Three of them have been named Amanda, and not one of those three has died in bed. By water, by fire, by the knife. An unlucky family."

"Evidently." James sipped his champagne.

"But you asked why I collected material. For a book—a photographic record, mainly. It begins with Anastasia, and traces all who are connected with her, relatives admitted and unknown, cousins many times removed, like ourselves." He ducked his head slightly to Amanda.

"Cousins ought to know each other," James said. "Your name is—"

"Summers. John Burlington Summers."

"This is Mrs. Rider. My name is James Paradine."

Summers was looking at Amanda. "The likenesses are remarkable. The family face survives."

"What will your book be called?"

"Just that. *The Family Face*, by John Burlington Summers. There is a subtitle: *A Study in the Physiognomy of Royalty.*"

"I shall buy a copy. Do you live here?"

"I live anywhere. London, Berlin, Sydney. For quite a while now in Sydney."

"I shouldn't have thought Valeta was a particularly good place for discovering descendants of Anastasia, even if you have struck lucky at the moment."

"I go anywhere I have a job to do."

"I expect you'd like a photograph for your dossier. And an outline of Mrs. Rider's ancestry."

"Very much indeed." Summers leaned toward Amanda. "I hope *you* won't be unlucky."

She got up. "I wish you'd both stop talking such bloody nonsense." She said to Summers, "I don't want to see any more of you. Keep out of my way or you'll be sorry. I'm going back."

Something about the way she spoke, some suggestion that James was bound to follow her, kept him in his seat. Summers looked after her. "You see the way she walks. Such arrogance. And that temper. All characteristic. Perhaps you should go after her."

"Perhaps I should. Tell me something I didn't understand. I never mentioned her name. How did you know she was called Amanda?"

The flat blue eyes looked at him. "I told you I was psychic. You don't think I'm serious about this? You don't believe me?"

"No."

"I'm staying at the Metropol. Come and see me."

6

Midnight. James sat at the table in his room, writing to Jerry. He felt, for no particular reason, extremely tired and kept yawning, but he was determined to get the events of the evening down on paper.

James Paradine Esquire, working hard on behalf of his old chum Jerry:
And when I say hard, I mean hard. Two letters one after another is a pace I certainly shan't keep up, but what's been happening here seems so fraught with oddity and apparent significance that I feel I must put it down. Just what it signifies I don't know—perhaps it's all in the imagination of somebody mixing up real life and detective fiction. And whether it's got anything to do with your inquiries into RR I have no idea. Either way, just write me a letter expressing extreme gratitude for all the trouble I'm taking.

Where to begin? First with Amanda, the second Mrs. R, much younger than tycoon husband. Had a drink with her in a café early this evening, and she said me da had tried to rape her in her room this afternoon. Said she'd been having an affair with him, had decided to stop it, he'd been angry. Confirmation: nasty marks on her neck. Contraindication: unlikelihood of my meek and mild father doing any such thing. Conclusion: it's a wise child who knows his own father. Haven't had a chance to talk to him yet. A says there'll be trouble if R gets to know about it, and I shouldn't wonder.

Now the plot thickens. While we were talking a man named Summers (he says) came up, talked a lot of nonsense about Amanda being a descendant of the Tsar's daughter Anastasia, seemed to be making some sort of threat or giving a warning. One of the local nuts? Then how did he know her name was Amanda when nobody had told him?

(Did you ask if I fancy A? Hum, well, ah. In a word, yes. But I should say she's poison.)

Does all this sound like moonshine, wasting a busy copper's time? What about RR? Well, he's as boring as I said, a back-slapping master of thunderous clichés. He told me my thesis was a waste of time—not far wrong, I daresay. Also tapped his forehead and said he hadn't got much up there, which may be accurate. But watching him with my dad, I can see that dad cringes before him emotionally, something that makes me pretty annoyed when dad's so much more intelligent and interesting. But I suppose what RR does have is a sort of animal power or magnetism. His relationship with dad contains quite a lot of love-hate on both sides, I should think.

Almost forgot to mention Sheila, the daughter. OK—rather nice, in fact. But too fat.

And now the field's clear for Uncle Hubert. Have I ever mentioned him to you, dad's elder brother? He's certainly the most colorful and interesting Paradine, which is not saying much. I remember his coming to stay when I was nine years old. Dad opened a cablegram, said "Hubert's out," and after a while I discovered this meant he was out of prison. Not an English prison, only in Africa, so you might say it didn't count too much against him. He'd been a cultural adviser to one of those black African republics, and after a change of regime they popped him in jail. Then there was the cable, and soon after that he arrived. I remember being fascinated by him—the funny smell of his clothes, which were patched and faded; his hair, which he wore clipped close to his head; his creaky voice, which sounded as if a door were being closed.

He stayed for three months. It turned out that he'd been treated splendidly in jail, because they were afraid the regime might change again. He brought a load of presents with him, including the carved head of an African rain god, which I've still got, but he had practically no money, and in retrospect I can see that he almost drove dad mad. For one thing, the housekeeper we had at the time hated him. He got up late, didn't eat meals at proper times, once or twice brought women back and they stayed the night. Imagine the morning confusion, the housekeeper going about tight-lipped, dad off to work in a terrible temper, Uncle H coming down to the breakfast room, where I was eating my cereal (he was installed when I came home for the school holidays), putting finger to lip, pouring *two* cups of coffee and taking them upstairs. It only struck me afterward, but I think subconsciously I realized then how essentially respectable and conventional my father was. Uncle H's whole life style was uncongenial to dad. I suppose really dad was a frustrated writer, and he'd like to have lived with Uncle H's freedom.

I liked Uncle H, but even I was relieved when he went off with some anthropological expedition to Nepal. He sent a parcel containing a shopworn sari for the housekeeper, a hookah for dad, who doesn't smoke, and a plastic air gun for me which came apart the first time I used it. After that I got a card every year for my birthday, sometimes with a present but always a card. Apart from that there was just the odd letter, one from Turkey, where he was with a trade mission, and another from Iran, where he said he was advising the Shah. In the last five years we'd hardly heard from him at all, just one brief note from Sydney, saying he thought he might stay there. I remember one phrase: "Have settled for commercial life like you!" He'd long since stopped sending me birthday cards, but he never forgot to say "Love to Jimmy," which was what he called me.

Well, you can see how amazing it is that he should turn up here. He looked just as I remembered, small like dad, but lively where dad is silent, hair cropped to his skull.

James put down his pen. He felt too tired to describe the whole evening at this length—and what was there in it, after all, except a lot of conjecture? He decided to finish the letter in the morning, brushed his teeth, got into bed and in a moment was asleep.

Hubert Paradine had arrived a few minutes after James's return from the Bar Central with Amanda. Roger and Geoffrey were back also from their trip in the speedboat, Roger making jokes about Geoffrey being surprised to find that the water was wet.

"Had to give him a good soaking to convince him, isn't that so, my old Geoff? Thought about tipping him in and leaving him to swim for it, then remembered he never managed to swim the length of the bath in the old days. Never mind, Geoff, have some whisky, it'll warm the cockles." Geoffrey said he was going up to have a bath. His host laughed uproariously. "You'll be getting into hot water. Just take care it isn't too hot, that's all."

To this as it seemed to James wholly unfunny remark his father made no reply, but went upstairs. Amanda had gone already. Roger and James were left alone.

There was the brisk toot-toot of a car's horn from the court-yard on the other side of the house. A few moments later a figure appeared at the end of the terrace, a small jaunty man with a few black hairs plastered down on the top of his head, a face rough and pitted as an outline map of hilly country, and wearing old clothes, in which he strutted with as much confidence as though they were smart and new. James recognized him immediately.

Hubert came forward grinning. His steps were short and he moved like a small boxer, almost dancing on his toes. "Mr. Rider, I'm Geoff's brother Hubert. You won't remember, but we met a long time ago, in Malbite Street."

"I remember." Roger took the offered hand. "Yes, I remember very well." He abandoned the hand and stood with his shoulders hunched, staring at Hubert, who did a smart half-turn to face James. "It isn't—it can't be—but it is," he said dramatically. "Little Jimmy. Well, well. Remember that model of Nelson's flagship I made you?"

James submitted to an embrace. His chin almost touched the top of Hubert's head. He remembered nothing about the model of Nelson's flagship. He asked how Hubert had found him.

"Came to England a couple of days ago, thought I've only got one brother, blood's thicker than water, I'll pay a visit. Called at Malbite Street, got address from Mrs. Whatever-her-name-is, said it was care of Rider. Rider, I thought, I know that name, it's Geoff's friend and employer Billy. Doesn't call himself Billy any more, though. Geoff and Billy, old friends together on holiday."

"What will you have to drink?" Roger asked. When Hubert said whisky, he went on. "So you came out here just to see Geoff again."

"Not altogether. Had a little business here. Coincidence, that. Funny thing about coincidences is they happen, ever noticed that?" Lowering his voice like one inquiring after an invalid, he said, "And how is Geoff?"

At that moment Geoffrey appeared. Hubert moved toward him, crying, "Brother!"

There could be no doubt about Geoffrey's astonishment. He looked at the figure advancing on him as though unable to believe in his existence. "What are you doing here?"

"Is that a way to greet a long-lost brother?" Hubert croaked, and then cawed with laughter. "Still the same old Geoff, isn't he? And I'm still the same old Hubert. People don't change, do they? They try to, but they don't."

He made it an open question, but nobody answered it. When Roger said that he must stay, Hubert showed no particular surprise. "Very kind of you. But I wouldn't want to impose."

"Plenty of room." Roger looked at Geoffrey, who stood frowning.

Hubert cawed again, slapped his small thigh. "Don't worry about Geoff, it takes him time to get adjusted to me. Anyway, I can't stay more than a couple of days. If you can put up with me for forty-eight hours—"

"Can't you stay longer?"

"No, then I'm off. Next week I'm seeing Hoo Flung Dung, the Chinese Health Minister, to discuss Peking's sanitary arrangements."

James winced. He had forgotten Uncle Hubert's rare but excruciating excursions into humor. The little man was standing with his back to his nephew, and it was impossible that he could have seen the wince, but now he swiveled, and fixed James with the stare of his bright eye. The look was unwavering and hard like a bird's, and a nod came at the end of it.

"Handsome. You want to look out for him. And look out for yourself, Jimmy, eh?"

"I try to, Uncle Hubert."

"So what are you doing with yourself?"

James told him. "What are *you* doing, Uncle Hubert? That's much more interesting."

"Just come from Australia. I had a few business interests there. I liked it. Liked the Australians too. Good businessmen. But I've given it up. I'll tell you what I'm here for, I've got plans for retirement."

Roger shook his head. "You don't want to retire. When people retire they just fade away."

"Like old soldiers. But I've got some plans laid. I'm not fixed on Spain, though. I might buy a little place near you, Geoff. After all, brothers ought to see each other. Wouldn't you like that?"

"I don't think you should retire," Roger repeated. "Not unless you've got a good pension."

Hubert looked as though he might say something more, but Amanda and Sheila appeared. In a moment he was on his feet, kissing their hands and talking about their beauty.

They ate in the garden, a fish dish flavored with garlic and saffron, red with prawns and black with mussels. Roger ate sparingly, Geoffrey hardly anything at all. Hubert, who had changed into white trousers and a nautical blue jacket with brass buttons, took a second helping. He disposed of the food with urgent speed, tearing the mussels free of their casings, crunching the prawns shell and all, although he spat out the toughest bits, and washing it down with frequent gulps of wine. At one moment he belched, loudly and unmistakably. Sheila thought him an awful little man, yet she found something attractive about him. He bore some resemblance to the Natural Man, who said and did just what he pleased without regard to other people. It was to be expected, after all, that the Natural Man's table manners might be a little crude. And it was fitting that for the Natural Man eating and drinking did not preclude conversation, and that he paid no regard to the convention that you should not talk while your mouth had food in it. She enjoyed the pleasure he seemed to take in needling his brother, and liked it still more when he provoked her father into losing his cool with Amanda.

"You've been working for Roger—how long is it now? Twenty years?" he asked.

Geoffrey did not reply. Roger said in his ponderous way, "Geoff doesn't work for me, he works with me."

"Ah. And how long's he been working *with* you?"

"I think it's fifteen years, isn't that so, Geoff?" Geoffrey muttered something that might have been agreement. "But the thing is that a company like BMS is really a cooperative enterprise. It can't be anything else. It's true I'm the Chairman, but power in BMS isn't invested in any individual. Alastair Stephenson is the Managing Director now, and his decisions would be my decisions."

"Suppose you didn't agree?" Hubert said. "Don't tell me you couldn't overrule him."

"I wouldn't do it," Roger said. "Team effort, that's the thing. There's no such animal as the indispensable man."

While James was pondering on whether there was anything significant about this exchange, Amanda at the other end of the table said, "Keep the lecture for the Rotary Club."

Roger stared at her. "You're supposed to look graceful at the end of a table, and you manage that very well. Just stick to it, otherwise you show your ignorance."

She dabbed her lips with her napkin, and spoke to Hubert. "I'm sorry about Roger. In the presence of anybody new he feels an urge to be even more boring than usual."

"Have I started something?" the Natural Man croaked. "Just as well it's a flying visit perhaps." He looked round, beaming.

"On my way to Peking. Then I might go back to Sydney. That's an interesting city. Anybody visited it? Pity, there's a lot to see, more than the bridge and the opera house. Much more. I might settle down there. Geoff, would that be a good idea?"

"If you settled anywhere that wasn't near me, it would be a good idea."

"Brotherly love," Hubert croaked, and rolled his eyes.

Amanda said gently, "Mr. Paradine, you and your brother obviously *don't* feel much love for each other, so why exactly are you here?"

For a moment Hubert seemed at a loss. He looked from Amanda to her husband, then laughed. "Only joshing, as the cardinal told the actress when she asked if he called that thing a miter. But really I've come over to fix up my retirement, that's a fact." In the next breath he asked, "Ever played the Game?"

"What do you mean, some kind of truth game?" James said. He was a great player himself of all kinds of games from piquet to complex word games.

"It's just called the Game. Calls for quickness of wits and a bit of acting ability. You might be good at it, Jimmy. We might try it." With a quick duck of his head to Roger he added, "If our host permits."

"Anything other people would like to do is all right with me."

So after dinner they played the Game in the drawing room, while drinking bitter black coffee prepared by Amanda. Hubert explained.

"Somebody thinks of a book, play, film or song title, then acts it out in mime and the others try to guess it. You can split up a word into syllables and indicate that you've done it, but you mustn't speak. I'll give you a sample."

He spread his hands to show it was a book title, held up two fingers for two words, then one to show that he was doing the first word, held it up again to show that this was the first syllable. He examined his blue jacket with care, holding it under the light.

"Blue," said Sheila. Hubert shook his head.

"Cloth. No, that wouldn't be the first syllable. Wool? Clothe?"

Amanda said, "Match . . . green . . . color." Hubert went on shaking his head, although at "color" he made an encouraging gesture.

James spoke for the first time. "Shade?" A head shake. "Tinge? Pattern—no, that's two syllables. Hue?" Hubert stopped him with upraised hand. "Hue is the first syllable?"

Hubert nodded, held up two fingers for the second syllable, pointed to himself, Geoffrey and Roger with nods, to Amanda and Sheila and shook his head.

"Man?" Amanda asked. He signified yes. "The first word's human?"

He nodded, held up two fingers for the second word, closed his eyes and began to grope around. His fingers touched Amanda's face.

"Human Blind Man's Buff?"

"*Human Bondage*," Sheila suggested. "Oh, that's got *Of* at the beginning, hasn't it?"

"*Human Feelings*," James said. "Dad's novel."

Hubert opened his eyes. "Right. I said you'd be good at it. Didn't think I'd remember your book, did you Geoff? Now one from you, young feller."

James had *Midnight Cowboy*, which was guessed by Amanda from his spirited rendering of falling off a horse. She had *Love Story*, in which she indicated love by putting her arms round James's neck. There was an odd little scene when her turn came round again. She had James Hilton's book and film *Lost Horizon*, which James guessed as soon as they got the word *Lost*. She asked how he had managed it.

"I don't know. Perhaps I've always wanted to live in Shangri-La."

"The only place to live." Her strangely colored eyes shone.

"But in the end one would get bored."

"Oh, would one?" she murmured, still looking at him.

Roger's voice was loud. "My love, you know you can go and

stay in Shangri-La any time you like. She saw it, wanted it, I bought it."

"I agree with James, I'd be bored in Shangri-La," Sheila said. "Nothing to do."

"Nonsense. You'd investigate the past, solve its problems." Roger was enthusiastic. "Solve the mystery of the nuraghi, find out who first came—"

"I don't want to talk about it any more," Amanda said languidly, and then to Roger in a tone so vicious that he looked quite startled, "So just shut up. Hubert, your turn."

Hubert opened his hands to show a book, held up four fingers. He did a before-and-after scene, and Sheila got the first word as *After*. An imaginary pile of things on the floor eventually gave them the second word as *Many*.

James had a flash of inspiration. "*After Many a Summer*. Novel by Aldous Huxley."

"He's bright. He's smart. He's got it." Hubert slapped James on the back, and then croaked, "Quotation, it's a quotation. I bet Geoff knows it."

Geoffrey Paradine stared at his brother. "I do, as a matter of fact. Tennyson. 'After many a summer dies the swan.' "

"Right. Good old Geoff the bookworm."

"I didn't know that," Roger said. "Not good at quotations."

" 'After many a summer dies the swan,' " Hubert repeated slowly, then moved into his cawing laughter, laughter that turned into a fit of coughing. His face grew red. He doubled up in a paroxysm, sank to the floor. A hoarse screeching sound came from his throat. Sheila knelt beside him, thumped him on the back. James ran out for water. Then it was over. Hubert sat up again, gasping like a man who has run a four-minute mile. The end of his nose was a chalky white. Sheila said, "You got too excited."

Roger's lumpy face was serious, almost solemn. "You want to bear that in mind. About excitement. I mean, it could be dangerous. You can't take it with you, that's very true. And excitement

—well, all excitement is bad for the old ticker."

Hubert looked up at him, still gasping a little.

Roger jingled coins in his pocket. "All this concentration on the Game has given me a headache. I'm going out. Nothing like sea breezes to blow a headache away."

Half an hour later they all went to bed. Hubert still looked pale, and was unwontedly silent. Roger had not returned.

Sheila found it hard to sleep. She thought of ingenious ideas she might have used in the Game, and then her mind turned to a young public-relations man she had gone around with for six months. She had broken things off because he talked all the time about media research. She found this boring, but it had also seemed to her that it was conduct alien to the Natural Man. It occurred to her that life would be much nicer if Natural Men like Hubert were more agreeable, and agreeable ones like James were more Natural. At this point, as though a curtain had been drawn, she fell asleep.

She slept until ten thirty, and woke with a headache. When she went downstairs only James was at the table. She poured coffee, refused food with a shudder.

"You look rather fragile. Did you sleep badly?"

"Like a log. I feel terrible."

"I'm a bit shagged myself. You didn't hear anything in the night?"

"I said I slept like a log. Should I have heard something?"

"I thought I heard a car, but probably I was dreaming. Uncle H has gone."

"Gone." She stared at him. "What do you mean?"

"My dear girl, I should have thought it was simple enough." He took another piece of bread, buttered it thickly, loaded it with a purplish substance. "You should try this tomato jam. Delicious. This morning he'd cleared out. Packed his things, taken his car, gone. And without leaving the smidge of a message. And nobody heard him go. Don't you call that odd?"

"Perhaps I will have something to eat, after all." She buttered some bread, ate a small piece experimentally. "If nobody heard him go, how do we know he's gone? I mean, why wasn't he left to sleep?"

"I woke up with a headache, saw his car had gone and asked Rodríguez where he was. He just shrugged, so I went up to his room. Bird flown. You're looking greenish. I hope you're not going to be sick."

"I feel better now I've eaten that bread. Thanks for your concern."

"I wonder if there's any cheese. I feel remarkably hungry." He rang the bell. Rodríguez appeared, his jowls bluer than usual. "Rodríguez, I know it isn't a Spanish specialty for breakfast, but I wonder if you have any cheese."

Rodríguez went out, returned with triangles of cheese wrapped in silver paper. He put them on the table, and looked at his watch before disappearing again.

"I think he'd like us to move from here. It's late."

"Stay where you are. Rodríguez is here to serve." He unwrapped two triangles, spread them on bread, bit. "Synthetic, I fear. I wonder if we were drugged."

"Don't be absurd."

"Not absurd at all. Both slept heavily, both have headaches. And I'll tell you something else. You're the only person who sleeps on the side of the house near the cars. Right? Uncle H wants to get away without anyone knowing. He slips a mickey finn into your coffee."

"And why does he put it in yours?"

"Because he knows my curious nature. Didn't you think the coffee was particularly bitter?"

"I did, now you come to mention it. But it was Amanda who poured the coffee."

"So it was."

"And anyway, why should he want to get away without anyone knowing?"

"Why should Uncle H have come here at all, when he and dad hate each other? Did you think there were currents seething away last night under the surface?"

Roger, wearing a scarlet and blue striped shirt that fitted his bulky body tightly, appeared in the doorway, evidently in high spirits. He beamed at them, began to sing:

"Oh, those who're late for breakfast
Shall be deprived of lunch.
While those who've done their duty
May munch and munch and munch.

I was in the pool before breakfast, I've taken out the speedboat, talked to the London office for ten minutes, fixed up for us to go to the corrida tonight—"

"Daddy, please. I'm not up to it this morning. My head aches. Does yours?"

"Not a trace of a headache. Come on, you sluggards."

They joined him on the terrace. Sheila sat in the shade and closed her eyes.

"Sheila heard nothing in the night," James said. Roger looked at him without comprehension. "Uncle Hubert's left. She slept on the other side of the house, but she didn't hear his car."

"Rodríguez told me he'd gone. He's a funny fellow, your uncle."

"Doesn't it seem strange to you?"

"Shouldn't be surprised at anything he did. Still, he might have left a note."

"Sheila's got a headache. I was suggesting that she might have been drugged."

Roger burst out laughing. "You've got a vivid imagination, my boy. Are you coming to this shindig tonight? Not really a corrida, of course, just a village imitation of Pamplona, but I think we ought to see it. Rodríguez's got seats for us on a cart."

James said to Sheila, "What you need is a brief immersion in the destructive element."

"The destructive element?"

"The sea."

When they came out he said, "Don't you feel better?"

"Yes. But then perhaps I would have done anyway."

"Your father was evasive about Hubert. Something odd's happening, and I wouldn't mind knowing what it is."

"You're very inquisitive." But perhaps inquisitiveness was a characteristic of the Natural Man.

Later James took his father for a drive. They went inland, on roads that corkscrewed up and up in a meaningless way, then corkscrewed down again. They passed peasants driving carts loaded with nuts, drove through what seemed deserted villages. They stopped in one of the villages, ate melon and tough beef, and drank the raw powerful local wine. James had been trying to screw up courage to speak to his father about Amanda, and with the second glass he managed it.

"Dad. Amanda said you've been having an affair. Is that true?"

His father gave up the beef, and smiled. "Does the idea shock you?"

"It did when she told me. Now I don't know. It isn't just that you're my father—"

"But that Roger's my oldest friend, is that it? I said he was partly responsible for Paula's death, but not how it happened. I should have told you long ago."

James heard the story incredulously. How extraordinary the behavior of one's parents and their friends seemed to have been, how complicated they always made things.

"You see that when the invitation was made, and it *was* an invitation, it was easy to give way."

"Yes. I see that. And now it's over?"

"She's made that very clear. When we came out here I was desperate. Couldn't bear the thought of being rejected—vanity, I suppose. Now that's over too. I've made up my mind." He smiled again. "Do you know, I think it's probably the first time in my life I've ever made up my own mind about something, instead of having it made up for me. Yesterday Roger said he wanted to move me from one department to another, and I agreed. But I shan't go."

"What are you going to do?"

"Today's Saturday. Tomorrow I shall tell Roger that this place doesn't agree with me, and I get migraine headaches here. Then I shall go home. I shall go back on Sunday or Monday." He added remorsefully, "I'm afraid this will make things awkward for you. I'm sorry about that."

"Think nothing of it, dad. I'm a free agent."

"When I've got back I shall retire. I shan't get as big a pension as I should in five years' time, but what does that matter? Why go on doing something you dislike when you don't have to? I can't think why I've stayed at BMS so long."

"What will you do, then?"

"I shall work for the breakthrough with the Paradine Defense." He sounded so much like a child looking forward to a treat that James felt he should sound a fatherly note of warning.

"You're quite sure you've finished with Amanda? Supposing she said yes again?"

"I should say no thank you," his father said with the utmost confidence.

The police came soon after they returned. They were all in the garden except Amanda. Geoffrey had his chessboard out, Roger was sprawled on a sun lounge, James and Sheila in the pool. Rodríguez brought out a small man wearing a gray-green uniform topped by a tricorne hat.

"Lieutenant Quevedo of the Guardia Civil. This is Señor Rider."

Roger struggled up, shook hands. "I thought this was the hour of the siesta."

The lieutenant said severely, "When there is work to do, there is no siesta."

"What can we do for you? Something about our cars?"

"Will you present me?"

Roger called, "Hey, Sheila, James!" They got out of the pool. "My daughter, Sheila. James Paradine. And this is his father, Geoffrey."

The lieutenant bowed, almost clicked his heels. "I am sorry to take you away from your swimming. That is the whole of your party?"

"My wife's upstairs, resting."

"Perhaps we may go inside? And perhaps you would wish to call your wife. And perhaps—" He glanced at Sheila's wasp-striped swimwear, and away.

"You want me to call Amanda? Is that necessary?"

"I think perhaps it is helpful."

Ten minutes later they were in the living room, Sheila wearing a sacklike yellow dress reaching to her ankles, Amanda virginal in white.

The lieutenant took out a notebook. "You have a friend named Princeton, Henry Princeton."

"Not so far as I know," Roger answered.

"He is not a friend of yours?"

"I don't know the name."

Quevedo was disconcerted. "It is my information that he has been staying here."

"Then your information would seem to be wrong."

"Perhaps." Dark eyes looked from one to another of them. "Señor Princeton is below medium height, thin hair—"

James sat up in his chair. "Uncle Hubert. Henry Princeton, Hubert Paradine."

"I do not understand. What does that mean?"

"His name is Hubert Paradine. He is my uncle, my father's brother. And he has been staying here."

"You will please describe this visit."

Before James could reply, Roger said heartily, "Lieutenant, before we go on, what about a drink? A drop of Scotch, or—"

"Thank you, nothing. You own this villa, I believe, Señor Rider. Will you please describe the visit?"

"Assuming it was Hubert Paradine, there's not much to describe. I hardly know him, but he's the brother of Geoffrey, over there. He turned up yesterday some time in the evening before dinner. He said he'd had to come out to Spain, wanted to see Geoff and James here because he hadn't seen them for a long time. Said he couldn't stay more than a couple of days, but he must have changed his mind, because this morning he'd packed his things and gone. I think that covers it." There was a murmur of agreement.

"At what time did he leave?"

"I'm telling you, we don't know. Rodríguez—you've seen him —gets up at seven thirty. The car had gone when he got up."

The lieutenant phrased his next question carefully, slowly. "Why did this gentleman leave so sudden? Did something happen to upset him while he was here?"

Amanda spoke for the first time. "He did a lot of needling of his brother."

"Needling?"

James cut in quickly. "Mrs. Rider means he said things that upset my father. But there was no quarrel, no quarrel at all."

He looked at his father, who said serenely, "Quite right. Hubert and I were beyond quarreling."

"Beyond quarreling, what is that?"

Geoffrey smiled. "It means we never saw each other. And I knew he would be here for only a couple of days."

Roger got to his feet and spoke forcibly. It was possible to see, James thought with interest, a glimpse of something steely that must lie beneath the surface of aimless good humor. "If we're going to say any more, lieutenant, I shall want to know what this is all about. What's your interest in Hubert Paradine, or whatever you call him? What's he done?"

Quevedo shut his notebook, snapped a rubber band round it. "This morning just after seven o'clock Corporal Santos of the

Guardia Civil was driving his motor scooter on a road just off the N232 highway between Castellón and Saragossa. About three kilometers from Morena he saw the marks of a car having left the road at a point where it is—'steep' is, I think, the word." His hand, cutting vertically, indicated steepness. "There were marks of it going over. He saw the car far below. It was burned. Inside it was a man in the driver's seat, of course dead. His papers showed him to be Mr. Henry Princeton." With a note of pride in his voice the lieutenant went on. "Corporal Santos reported back to his post. A report was passed on to Castellón de la Plana. It was established there that the car had been hired from Valencia. The hirer asked the distance to Valeta, and mentioned the Villa Victoria."

There was silence. Poor Uncle Hubert, James thought, all that scurrying eagerness ended by a car going over a hillside in Spain. Amanda lighted a cigarette and offered one to Quevedo, who shook his head. He had a slightly self-satisfied air, as though he expected praise for the speed with which the Guardia Civil had discovered the dead man's association with the villa. Roger sighed. A bromide is on the way, James thought. He was not wrong.

"In the midst of life, as they say. Very sad. Tragic."

"Tragedy," the lieutenant confirmed. He took out a packet of small cigars, asked permission to smoke, lighted one. The pungent odor hung on the afternoon air.

"I suppose it was misty and he went too near the edge. Perhaps a skid."

Quevedo shook his head. "No skid."

"Then how did the accident happen?"

"Perhaps an accident, perhaps not. That he should travel not under his own name, that is strange."

"Was his passport in the name of Henry Princeton?" James asked.

"That is so. We shall see. In Castellón the doctors—" He indicated something being cut up.

"A post-mortem," James suggested. "Opening up the body."

"Precisely. The night was clear, no fog. I do not see why the car should have left the road. Perhaps it is all nothing. Very possibly. It is simply that we investigate, you understand. The Guardia Civil is efficient, everything is investigated."

The lieutenant got as close to a smile as at any time during the interview. Before leaving he said, almost as an afterthought, that he would like Geoffrey to come to Castellón to identify the dead man. Not now—he was not returning to Castellón immediately; he would telephone later.

James said to his father, "I can do it, if you like."

"No, I'll see the last of Hubert. He was always a trouble, and it's not to be expected that he should end any other way."

James Paradine felt afterward that the events of that day should have been printed on his memory indelibly. For somebody preoccupied with the interaction of real life and fiction, this was all surely ideal material. The discovery of Uncle Hubert's departure, the visit of the stiff little policeman, and the day's later events must have generated tensions. But in fact if these existed, they were not on display.

His father seemed perfectly composed, even when James had asked him, "You didn't have a great row with Uncle Hubert after we'd gone to bed, did you? I mean, I don't understand what made him go off like that."

"No, I didn't have a row. I feel asleep at once."

"And woke with a headache?"

"As a matter of fact, I did. Why are you so interested? Hubert was a bad man, that's what you don't seem to understand. I know it's an old-fashioned phrase, but it does apply to him."

"You're sure you don't want me to go in and identify him?"

"No, I owe him that." And when Quevedo telephoned from the comisaria at Castellón, Geoffrey went off in the car. He refused James's offer to go with him. "No, thank you. I'd sooner be alone."

James said nothing more, but Roger protested. "You're going to miss all the jollification. María's prepared a hamper to make your mouth water. I tell you what—pick us up in Valeta after you've looked at him."

After his father had gone, James went to his room, added a long postscript about Hubert's disappearance and death to his letter to Jerry, and went out to post it. As he left the villa he saw the motorboat puttering about on the sea, among the buoys placed to mark the channel from the beach. When he returned, the boat was being drawn up. Rodríguez jumped out of it. He looked up, saw James, grinned. Was the grin that of one football fan to another, or was there something contemptuous about it?

The depósito de cadáveres was out of the center of the town, a squat gray building in a street full of factories.

Quevedo was apologetic. "I am sorry, this is not a pleasant place. You are not nervous?"

"I don't think so."

The lieutenant's heels rang on the marble floor. They went through a room with a pair of bored-looking clerks in it. Then there was what Geoffrey thought of as the hospital smell. He remembered being taken to see his mother in a hospital. She was having an operation for some mysterious illness, which he only later learned was a hysterectomy. He had been fourteen. Hubert had got a job in a small theater company and was away touring up in the north of England. He said that he had not received the telegram telling him about the operation. His mother wept bitterly because of Hubert's absence, and Geoffrey had always believed that his brother had ducked out of this responsibility, as he had ducked out of others during his life.

"Here we are."

The strip lighting illuminated a bare high room. It was cold. The attendant was a shuffling little old man in a frayed blue uniform with bits of gold on the sleeves. At each side of the room was a white porcelain table. Quevedo nodded toward one.

"There we do the opening of the bodies. In this case, tonight."

Geoffrey nodded. Around the room were what looked like big filing cabinets with handles on them. The attendant pulled one of these handles, and a drawer came out on rollers. It was empty.

A burst of explosive speech from Quevedo. The man muttered something. Shuffled across the room, looked at a piece of paper, came back, pulled the handle of another drawer.

What would be revealed? Geoffrey had a vision of his mother lying in one of those drawers, a feeling that the rollers as they slid back would reveal her body, terribly naked as he had never seen it. As the drawer opened he closed his eyes. It was only with an effort that he refrained from crying out.

"Señor Paradine." The rat-a-tat of Quevedo's voice brought him back. Hubert lay there, naked. The body was meager as Geoffrey's own, the legs, like his, surprisingly hairy. One side was discolored by burning, but the face, Hubert's face with its beaky nose and thin cheeks, was unmistakable. The mouth had fallen open, giving the face a foolish expression.

He said, "That is my brother." The drawer was pushed back.

Back at the comisaria, in a small office with a photograph of Franco on the wall, Quevedo offered Geoffrey a glass of some sweetish anise liqueur.

"I thank you for coming. It must be for you most painful."

"I told you that my brother and I didn't see each other. I hadn't seen him for years."

"So this visit, it was unexpected. Why should he have made it, if you are not friendly?"

"I don't know."

"And then his going, that was unexpected too. But you say you had no quarrel."

"No quarrel."

"And you have no idea why your brother should leave suddenly in the night or the early morning. You heard nothing?"

"I have no idea. And I heard nothing."

"It is strange that when his car started up at—who knows?—one, two, three o'clock, nobody heard it."

"Not very strange. There's only one bedroom on that side of the house."

"It is a mystery. You are not interested to solve it, I think."

"I've told you my brother and I weren't friendly. We didn't like each other. But we weren't enemies."

On the wall opposite Franco a photograph showed a group of Guardia Civil giving the fascist salute as they marched past a stand in what looked like a military parade. Quevedo got up, went across to this picture.

"This is our parade after being accepted into the Guardia. Seven years ago. Here you see me." Geoffrey got up and went over to the picture. Quevedo pointed to a tricorne-hatted figure indistinguishable from the others. "Our training is very strict, like the army. We are the police army, you understand. We are responsible to the Minister of the Interior, you understand, not the Director of Police."

"I see."

"It is a fine thing to be a lieutenant in the Guardia Civil. A position of importance in the state. I thank you for coming, Señor Paradine. When the investigation is complete, we shall be in touch again." He shook hands gravely, sketched a bow.

7

The corrida was at the other end of the village. Sheila walked in with James. The others came in cars, Roger and Amanda in one, Rodríguez and María in the other. Sheila was wearing a distinctly tight, low-cut green cotton dress, with what she had always regarded as extremely nice green-and-gold sandals. She expected some comment from James, but she might have been naked, for all the attention he paid to her. He walked silently by her side in the dusty road, head down, long hair curling at the back of his neck. What was he thinking about? If she *were* naked, of course, he would have to notice, although even then perhaps he would turn away in revulsion from her figure because it didn't look like that of his boyfriend back in England. She decided to make this point. He chose the same moment to speak, and her "If I were naked—" was lost in his words.

"After many a summer. Don't you think that's odd?"

With exaggerated surprise she said, "You've noticed."

"Noticed what?"

"That I'm here."

"Sorry. Did you say something? Before that, I mean."

"It doesn't matter. What's odd?"

"Hubert wasn't the sort of man who knew quotations from Tennyson. Or even the titles of Aldous Huxley novels. So I wondered, why don't we call on him?"

"Call on who?"

"John Burlington Summers, Bachelor of Arts and expert on the Grand Duchess Anastasia. I told you about meeting him when I was out with Amanda. He invited me to call. This is where he's staying."

They were standing by a bead-curtained doorway. A sign in faded blue lettering said METROPOL. They went in.

There was a smell of stale cooking oil. They were in a dark hall with a small reception desk in it. Chairs, walls and reception desk were deep brown in color.

James called out twice, then pressed a light switch and produced a ghostly illumination from a group of small twisted-candle lamps. He opened a door, peered in, reported, "Dining room. Nobody there. Gone to the corrida. But Summers may be here." He went behind the reception desk, came up with a book.

"What are you doing?"

"Visitors' book. They often put the room number in it when visitors sign in."

"Suppose somebody comes back."

"They should have been on duty. Scandalous neglect. Here it is—J. B. Summers, Room Five. Come on."

She followed him reluctantly up the deep-brown staircase. At the top a passage stretched to left and right. James found another light switch, walked along the passage, made a thumbs-up sign. He pointed to the number *5* as she joined him, tapped on the door, then knocked firmly.

The smell of oil was now blended with a smell of garlic. He turned the handle of the door, and it opened. She gave a brief yelp.

"I don't think we should—"

But James was already inside. "Somebody's been here already."

The room was more comfortable than the dismal nature of the hotel suggested. There was a bed, a small writing table, a chest of drawers and a large wardrobe, all except the bed in dark, heavily carved mahogany. The shutters were drawn against sunlight. The room was in disorder. The chest of drawers was open and the clothes inside had been turned over. The bed had been stripped. The wardrobe doors were open. A pile of books and papers lay on the table. James crossed to an interior door, hesitated a moment and then flung it open, to reveal a small bathroom.

"Nobody." He looked in the chest of drawers, then turned to the wardrobe. "One suit, one pair of shoes. He travels light, does old J.B."

"You really enjoy this, don't you?"

"I suppose I do. I'm a student of crime, you know."

"Suppose he comes back. Let's get out."

"I've told you, he invited me to come and see him. So here I am. This is interesting. He wasn't kidding about his interest in the Tsar and Anastasia." He had picked up some books from the table, and she saw the titles: *The End of the Romanovs; I Am Anastasia; The Untold Story of the Russian Royal Family; Pretenders to the Throne.* "And he really wrote about them too." He showed her a bundle of manuscript beside the books, the edges badly dog-eared. "Chapter One, 'The Flight of the Romanovs, a New Witness.' Chapter Two, 'Did the Tsar Die in Exile?' Chapter Three, 'Some False Anastasias and My Own Links with the Russian Royal Family.' And that's about it. Apart from that, only lots of notes."

"What do you think has happened?"

"Obviously, somebody knew Summers would be out, and did over his room. It looks as though they found whatever they were looking for. The books and papers on the table here have hardly been disturbed."

"Clever."

"Fantastic." He waved a hand, and she could not help noticing that it was thinner and more delicate than her own. "A virtuoso of the obvious, that's me."

"What do you think's happened to him?"

"Your guess is as good as mine. He kept some stuff in the wardrobe, as well as these papers on the table." He cleared a space, took out a pile of papers and magazines from the wardrobe and drew up a chair.

"You can't do that. He might walk in at any minute."

"I'll chance it. If you want to leave—" She shook her head. "Then you might as well look through some of these. It shouldn't take more than five minutes."

"What am I looking for?"

"How do I know? The odds are that anything interesting has gone already."

He gave her some of the papers, and she began to look through them. Most of them were newspaper accounts of interviews with people who said they had met some members of the Russian royal family in Florence or Bangkok, or working on an Israeli kibbutz. There was an article on the possible curing of hemophilia, from which the Tsarevitch had suffered, letters and memoranda ("Find out name of Ekaterinburg station master"), bills for hotel accommodation. It was when unfolding one of the cuttings that she found the letter. Or, rather, the fragment torn from a letter, rather less than a half-sheet. She read:

. . . I don't think it will do for this one to be like Swan. No doubt you'll think of something. It has to be unobtrusive. Anyway, R wants to see you, and will give all details himself. The name is Amanda . . .

She handed it to James. He read it, then put it down. His face was pale.

"What's the matter?"

"I know the writing. Uncle Hubert. He used to send me a Christmas card every year." He read it again, said softly, "And after many a summer dies the swan. What odds would you give that this particular Swan is dead? And who's the one that isn't to be like Swan? Amanda?"

When they left the hotel the reception desk was still empty. The street was packed with cars and people. It was growing dark. They made their way toward the corrida.

8

"The men look nice, but when will something happen?" Amanda asked.

Carts had been drawn up round the four sides of a small plaza, so that all the entrances were blocked to traffic. The carts were tightly lashed with ropes, and chairs and benches had been put on them. The whole population of Valeta seemed to be on these carts, with small children and babies very conspicuous. A few tourists jumped on the carts too, but were briskly ordered down by the Spanish occupants. The Riders' cart had half a dozen chairs on it. Rodríguez stood among the crush of people on the ground, wearing a suit in purple plum color, dissuading boys from jumping onto the empty chairs. Opposite to them, what was presumably the local brass band played furiously. Behind the band, people were jammed in and around the doors of a café.

"Patience." Roger was conspicuous in a scarlet toweling shirt dotted with blue stars. "Mañana is the motto in Spain. Can I have some more chicken?"

She passed a chicken leg from the hamper and sat, chin in hand, looking down at the boys and girls talking and joking in the middle of the square.

"There's James. And Sheila too." She waved at them. The band struck up a new tune.

"Is that 'Onward, Christian Soldiers'?" He began to bellow: "Onward, Christian soldiers, marching as to war." He broke off. "There he is."

"Geoffrey?"

"The bull."

At one end of the square a rough wooden barricade had been put up, with an improvised gate. This had been drawn aside, and a young bull pushed out into the square. He stood there, head up and tail swishing. Then, frightened by the thunderous sound that greeted his appearance, he turned back and tried to get out. Whacked at with sticks, he turned again into the plaza, took a few hesitant steps, stood still. Half a dozen adventurous young men came within a few yards of him, jeering and waving red dusters or handkerchiefs. The bull turned away from them and trotted round his end of the plaza, trying to find an exit.

"Big deal," Amanda said in mock American.

James and Sheila were making their way through the crowd. James began to wriggle through a space between cartwheels.

"What are you doing?"

"Going the quickest way across the square." He crawled under a protective dashboard, and emerged into the plaza. A bearded young man slapped him on the back and offered him a porrón. James raised it, directed the thin stream of wine accurately down his throat. If I'd tried to do that, half of it would have gone on my dress, Sheila thought. He called, "Come on."

There was not much space between the carts, and at one point she became almost totally stuck. She was aware that he was watching her progress with amusement. Crawling under the dashboard was not easy, and she felt something tear.

"Well done."

"No need to be so bloody sarcastic. I've ripped this dress."

He examined it. "Nothing serious. Look out."

The bull was galloping in their direction. Perhaps insults had had their effect, perhaps a judicious stone or two had been thrown—he was certainly on the move. Young men and women scattered with shouts of joyful fear, swinging up onto the sides of the carts out of range. James and Sheila found themselves at the tag end of a group. She had a vision of her body impaled on the horns, tossed in the air, trampled. She stumbled and screamed. Then her arm was savagely wrenched so that she was pulled sideways, she was beside a dashboard, sheltered by James's body, and the bull had gone past. He thundered to the other end of the plaza, lifted his head and gave a mournful cowlike moo.

"There's no need to look as though you've just saved a helpless cripple," she said. "Or to wrench my arm off. I slipped, that's all, but I'd have got away. He wouldn't have tossed me."

"You're right there. He hasn't got any horns. They only use young bulls for this sort of caper. You weren't in too much danger, I agree." He pulled her to him and kissed her in a brotherly manner on the cheek. Together they ran across the plaza. James jumped onto the cart, gave her a hand up.

"We got lost," she said.

James was suddenly aware of hunger. Amanda passed him a bowl of shelled prawns in a savory sauce.

The unsatisfactory bull was allowed to retire, among jeers from the crowd. He was replaced by a more mettlesome black animal, which was accompanied into the plaza by a man on a horse, wearing cardboard armor and carrying a bamboo lance with which he prodded the bull. The bull turned and made for him, but the horseman easily moved aside. The bull dashed on, drew up beside a group of carts, turned.

"They liven up as it goes on, Rodríguez tells me," Roger said. "I'm just going to see a man about a dog. And I may walk round a bit. If you want to go back, don't wait for me." He stepped down from the cart, spoke to Rodríguez and started pushing a way through the crowd.

A corporate gasp, then a long sigh came from the people on the carts. Two boys and a girl had got near to the bull. He charged them, knocking down one of the boys, then the girl. The boy rolled over and over, jumped up to demonstrate that he was unhurt, clasped his hands above his head. The horseman jabbed the bull with the bamboo lance to distract him. The bull butted the horse. The knight half fell, half jumped off, then leaped on the back of the bull and rode him triumphantly. The gate was opened and bull and rider charged through it, followed by the horse. Fifty people rushed to the girl on the ground, but she got up unaided. There was applause as she was escorted to a cart and given some wine. She waved to the crowd as she drank it.

Strings of lights came on, twinkling over the plaza. Round the band there was a circle of them, so that it appeared to be framed in red, blue and green. As it struck up again, another bull entered the square, this time accompanied by two figures, both dressed in scarlet and white, one on stilts. The smaller one performed cartwheels almost under the bull's nose; the other walked around uncertainly, occasionally raising a very tall conical hat. The bull remained apathetic.

Amanda yawned. "This is becoming too much like a circus. Is anybody going to walk back with me?"

Her remark was aimed at James, who said that he was staying for a while. Sheila said that she would stay too. It was eight thirty when Amanda set off on the way back to the villa. As bull succeeded bull, however, and the band played more enthusiastically, and the locals grew more daring in their treatment of the animals, James's enthusiasm faded, and soon after nine they left, driven back by Rodríguez in his purple suit. "Not like the futbol," he said to James, "I think the futbol his more hexciting." James agreed.

When they returned, Geoffrey had just come back. He explained that the car had stalled mysteriously a mile out of Castellón, and that he had had to walk to a nearby garage to get them to come and put it right. Roger, however, did not return. It was midnight before they thought that there might be something odd about this, and not until Sunday morning was the word "disappearance" used. In the end Amanda rang the police.

9

To be a lieutenant in the Guardia Civil was undoubtedly a fine thing, as Lieutenant Quevedo had said to the little Englishman, but there were times when he felt his authority to be a burden. To be telephoned just before midnight on Saturday by Dr. Santana with details of the post-mortem findings on the dead man Princeton or Paradine was bad enough, but he decided that no action need be taken until Monday. On Sunday morning he went to mass as usual, and he was making preparations for a visit to his wife's family in Valencia—a visit for which he wore his ceremonial uniform, although he was not strictly supposed to do so, a blue tunic and trousers, with an elegant black felt tricorne faced with gold—but when the telephone call came from the comisaria to say that Señor Rider had apparently vanished, he knew that something had to be done. Wearily, disgustedly, he took off his ceremonial uniform and put on his usual gray-green jacket and trousers. He told his wife that she must go alone to Valencia and that there she was to impress upon her brother the supreme importance of the duties entrusted to her Francisco, and went in to the station.

Installed in his office, the lieutenant rang the villa. When he put down the receiver he recognized that the affair was out of his hands. He felt both sorry and relieved, sorry because he felt that he had impressed the English with an idea of the efficiency and alertness of the Guardia Civil, and relieved because although

Lieutenant Quevedo wished more than anything to become Captain Quevedo, he knew that the way forward did not lie through a criminal affair involving the English, and this case looked very much as though it might be that. In such a matter, anyway, he had no choice. The affair, with its suggestion that a major crime might have been committed, was no longer a matter for the Guardia Civil, but for the DIC. Quevedo accordingly telephoned the Policía Armada y de Tráfico, and asked to speak to Señor Galera. He was told that Galera was at home, but that if the matter was important he could be telephoned there. When he rang, Galera asked, as Quevedo had known he would, that the lieutenant should come out himself. His Sunday was ruined.

Manuel Galera, Jefe de Servicio in the Departamento de Investigación Criminal, or DIC, was a big untidy man in his early forties, with a shock of gray hair that he never bothered to brush properly. Like other Spanish plainclothes policemen, he had attended a special school for legal and political instruction, after completing his course at the State Police Training School. The instructor's report on Galera had said that he was clever but lacking in proper respect for state authority, and too fond of engaging in arguments about the nature and uses of power to be regarded as reliable in the investigation of political offenders. He was employed therefore as a crime investigator without political responsibility, a fact that limited his opportunities and had delayed his promotion. There was a time when he had been bitter about this and had hoped for a change of government attitude, a time even when he had thought of leaving Spain, but all that was in the past. Today he had his agreeable wife María and two beautiful children, and for most of the time he was content.

He was still impatient with the political stupidity of a regime which used its police to spy on any student group gathered in a private house to discuss the possibility of mild liberal reforms, but was poorly equipped with the tools of forensic medicine necessary to deal with a crime of any subtlety. He had once been sent to Britain on an exchange course, and had been deeply impressed by the sophisticated tools and methods he had been shown. When he asked questions about the possibility of bringing such sophistication to his own country, he was told that it would cost too much, and also that it was unnecessary. It was true that in Spain few violent crimes were subtle, but Galera had always hoped that he would encounter one.

Galera's villa was in the hills, a few kilometers out of town. Several things about the Jefe de Servicio annoyed Quevedo—his untidiness, a general air of lacking proper regard for rank and authority, the fact that his clothes always looked rather shabby and slovenly—and these things added up to a distrust of the man. The lieutenant was ready to acknowledge in principle that it was advisable for members of the DIC to wear plain clothes, but in reality he believed that anybody in authority ought to appear in a uniform. How otherwise could people know that he should be paid proper respect? Quevedo suspected Galera of being an atheist, and suspected him also of sympathy for milk-and-water liberals. But it was to Galera that he had to report, and so he properly reported, sitting severely upright on a metal garden chair.

They were in the shade of a small patio. Galera cracked nuts, dissected and ate them, drank sherry. The lieutenant had taken a glass of sherry, but it was too dry for his taste.

"So the dead man had been taking drugs. Or they had been given to him. Did Santana say what drug?"

"Some kind of sedative, nothing harmful. A precise identification is not possible."

Not in Spain, Galera thought. He said aloud, "So he might have been given this drug during the evening, taken from the villa in a drugged sleep, driven to the place where he was found, put at the wheel of his car and sent over the hill. What happened, then, to the man who did it? The car was searched for prints?"

"The car was burned. Only by chance was the body preserved."

"It was not searched for prints? Oh, Lieutenant Quevedo." Galera shook his head. "But you looked, of course, for the other car."

"The other car?"

Galera said patiently, "If there was another man, how did he get away? It may be that he walked and was picked up afterwards. If so, he will very possibly have been seen. But if, as you seem to think, somebody at the Villa Victoria may have been responsible, then probably he was in another car. This would mean that two people were involved, one driving the car with the drugged man in it, the other ready to take back the driver."

Quevedo said sullenly, "There was no reason to suppose anything except an accident."

"You did not look for the tire marks of another car? Or inquire about a stranger in the district?"

"The proper inquiries were made. And I looked at the tire marks of the car that went over, to see if it had skidded. I should have noticed the marks of another car."

"Very well. We all act within the limits of our capacities. We will put an inquiry about this Paradine who calls himself Princeton through Interpol. Now tell me about the other English at the villa, especially the one who has disappeared."

While Galera went on cracking nuts and drinking sherry, Quevedo told him. During the recital he noticed that Galera's trousers were very dirty, that two of his fly buttons were undone, and that he was wearing some sort of carpet slippers. These things disgusted him.

10

To visit the English, Galera put on a suit and exchanged the carpet slippers for shoes, but he remained a rumpled untidy man who looked fatter than he was. He talked to the servant Rodríguez Orantes, whose appearance struck some distant chord in his mind, and then went into the living room. The people in it sat around, looking as though they were waiting for something to happen.

Galera believed in the value of first impressions. They represented the immediate impact of a personality, and although they were sometimes hopelessly wrong, they were often valuable. On this occasion he was much struck by Amanda Rider. A beauty, undoubtedly, but also surely a born liar, lecher, troublemaker—he had known a murderess with those bright shallow eyes. Geoffrey he summed up as a little man wrapped up in himself, not the kind of man likely to commit an act involving physical violence. The two younger people—well, the young woman was plump, the young man strikingly handsome. Otherwise, they did not make an immediate impression.

He was struck by the calmness with which the wife, or widow, asked if he had been in touch with hospitals.

"Señor Rider has not been taken to a hospital—that has been checked. I have two men now in Valeta trying to find whether he was seen after he left the corrida last night. This is a shock for you," he said to Amanda, although she showed no sign of shock. "Do you have any idea where your husband may be?"

"No. Why should you think so?"

"You seem so very unworried. Perhaps he gave you a hint that there might be trouble, something like that? Or that he might have to go away for a time?"

"No hint at all. But Roger can look after himself. I'm sure he'll come back. It was Sheila here who thought I should ring you."

"You don't think he has been picked up, robbed and beaten, then killed? Even in Spain such things happen."

She said in a low voice, "No. You're trying to upset me."

"You think he disappeared of his own accord, eh?"

"I don't think anything."

"You are very restrained. A man goes away at eight o'clock to fulfill a natural function and look round the village. Why does he not return? There are three possibilities. One, he went away of his own accord, he intended to go. Two, he meets unexpectedly somebody he knows, or who knows him, and is given information so important that he leaves. Three, he has been attacked, injured, kidnapped. Which of these three is most likely?"

He looked round, comfortably smiling. Geoffrey Paradine shook his head, Amanda stayed impassive, Sheila looked at James. Galera went on.

"And what connection has this disappearance with the death of Señor Hubert Paradine, who was under sedation and probably not conscious when he died?"

James spoke, "You mean he wasn't driving the car?"

"Almost certainly he was not driving the car."

"There's something else you should know. Another man has disappeared."

The detective listened to his story of the visit to Summers. "One death, two disappearances. It would be surprising if there were not a link between them, eh?"

"This man Summers was a nut. Anything may have happened to him," Amanda said.

"A nut?"

"A crank," James said. "He had this fixed idea about the Russian royal family. He thought they'd escaped from Russia. He said he was descended from them, and that Mrs. Rider was too. I thought he was threatening her."

Amanda said sharply, "Nonsense. I daresay he's come back by now."

"We shall find out." Galera got up.

Geoffrey spoke for the first time. "I want to go back to England. I was going to tell Roger tomorrow. Is that all right?"

"I am sure it will be all right, as you say. But it is possible I may have some further questions. My employers are not generous, they prefer that I should talk to you here and not fly over to England." He flapped his arms, smiling amiably. "I hope I shall not keep you very long."

"You're saying we can't go home."

"Today is Sunday. Ask me that question tomorrow evening, better still on Tuesday. Who knows, perhaps tomorrow Señor Rider and Señor Summers will both have returned. And now, if perhaps you have a photograph?"

He left with a couple of snaps of Roger Rider which were said to be recognizable likenesses.

11

The case was a difficult one to handle, Galera thought on his return to headquarters, partly because he was not sure whether any case existed. Perhaps Hubert Paradine had been driving the car and had fallen asleep at the wheel. Perhaps Rider and Summers would return. But if a crime had been committed involving one or more of these Englishmen, things would not be easy. The degree of cooperation he could expect would be strictly limited.

It was for the Spanish police, and not for those of another country, to find out the answers to those questions. The help given from Britain and elsewhere would be confined to information, and if he wanted detailed inquiries made in a foreign country, that would involve problems.

Nevertheless, the affair gave promise of being the subtle complicated case on which he had always wanted to test himself. He rang María, told her that he would not be home until very late and settled down to work. During the next ten hours, until two o'clock on Monday morning, he gathered information. He asked Interpol for anything they could give him about Paradine-Princeton and about Summers; sent an agent into Valeta to see if Summers had returned, and if he had, to bring him in for questioning; received the report of Suarez, the agent who had been trying to find out how and when Rider disappeared; sent a cable to New Scotland Yard. During the couse of all this, just after ten o'clock in the evening, he had a meal of mixed fried fish sent in from a nearby restaurant, and washed it down with raw white wine. He also drank several small cups of strong black coffee. Late on Sunday night he collated and summarized the information he had gathered, something that he enjoyed doing, and knew he did well. And on Monday he was back in the office again at nine thirty to explain the exact situation to Colonel Félix Prieto, who was in charge of the whole area.

The first report to come in was from Suarez. The agent had found two people who remembered seeing Rider after he left the plaza. Both said that he seemed to be wandering idly along the Rua San Nicolau, Valeta's principal street. The time then was approximately eight thirty. After that, he had vanished. Suarez had spoken to a clerk in the post office who had seen a car stop on the main road, a few meters away from him. A man had got into it, and from the description he might have been Rider. The driver, another man, had driven off in the direction of Valencia. The clerk had little interest in cars, and remembered about this one only that it was green. He had no idea of make, nor of what the driver looked like, except that he was a man and "about my age," which was thirty-five.

Marni, the agent who investigated Summers, had discovered that he had not slept in the Metropol on Friday night. On Saturday morning his bed had not been used. Apart from that, the hotel owner knew little about his guest. Summers had arrived five days earlier, and had taken the room for a week. He had paid in advance, had only one visitor, been no trouble. The visitor had come on Friday night fairly late, after ten o'clock at night. The owner's wife had caught a glimpse of the man, and described him as big, a hard brutal face, not unlike Summers himself to look at, a typical Englishman. She was shown the snaps of Rider, but could not be sure whether he was the man.

So far the information from Valeta.

Galera had sent through a request to Madrid to know whether Rodríguez Orantes and the woman María had criminal records. The reply had come late in the evening. Nothing was known against María, but Rodríguez had served two prison sentences, one of two years and one of three, for robbery with violence. He had been employed in service by other employers, and his last conviction had been in 1967.

Information from Interpol came in before midnight, through the National Central Bureau in Madrid, to Galera's pleasure and surprise. But then Interpol, that vast filing cabinet, was incalculable. There were occasions when you ran an inquiry through them and the results did not come in for a week, and then were far from complete. At another time, like this one, the response was speedy and efficient enough to make one sure that Interpol was indispensable.

The information in the radio messages relayed from Madrid was important. John Burlington Summers was probably fifty-two years old. He was English, educated at Rugby. He had not been to a university. He had had a distinguished war career during which he had reached the position of Lieutenant-Commander, RNVR. After the war he had served a twelve-month sentence in Britain for demanding money with menaces, and one of five years in Paris for the attempted murder of a liquor merchant. It was suggested that Summers had been hired by another liquor firm to intimidate their rival, but this had not been proved. He had appeared in the Congo as a member of Mike Hoare's army of mercenaries and had been possibly involved in the death of Lumumba. From 1965 onward he had been in Sydney, Australia, where he had been employed by a gambling syndicate. It was suspected that the syndicate used him as a strong-arm man to put pressure on backers who welshed on their debts. He was suspected of having beaten up several people, but nobody would give evidence against him. He had not been charged with any offense in Australia.

The information about Hubert Charles Paradine, alias Henry Porter, Henry Princeton, and a couple of other names, was scantier but still interesting. Hubert had been part of several trade missions and advisory organizations that were suspected of being a cover for smuggling drugs in Turkey and North Africa, arms in Iraq and Belgium. He had been in prison in Africa, and briefly in Belgium, and had been charged with blackmail in Australia in 1968, although the charge was dropped. His career differed from that of Summers in that he had never been charged with any offense involving violence. It resembled Summers' in the fact that he had lived in Sydney since the late Sixties working for a firm called Intertrade, which appeared to be the selling end of another firm called Austro-Asian Products. Nothing was known against Paradine during his years in Australia.

The radio telegrams gave little personal information about either man, although they said that Summers had been twice married and divorced, and that Paradine had no known personal attachments. The message did not say anything about Summers' Romanov interests, which from the papers in his room appeared to be genuine. Nor did it describe the work Paradine had been doing for Intertrade, or whether this was a cover for some other activity. In two or three days Galera would get much fuller information in the form of a "circulation" from Interpol, which would give the physical characteristics of the two men, together with their fingerprints and more details about their activities. Or at least he could have all this if he wanted it. And he could have more information from New Scotland Yard, which had simply told him so far that none of the party at the villa had a criminal record. He could talk to his friend Inspector Lawton of the Yard on the telephone, renewing old acquaintance; he could talk to the Australian police in Sydney. The question was whether the colonel would authorize it.

Colonel Félix Prieto was a dark neat man who wore rimless glasses and smelled of aftershave. He was DIC commander in the whole of the Levant. Galera knew that the job should have belonged to him, although he knew too that he would not have been able to endure the administrative work involved for more than a week. He regarded Prieto as another Quevedo, a machine bureaucrat without imagination. And so it proved. When he heard about telephone calls to New Scotland Yard and to Sydney, Prieto pursed his little boxlike mouth.

"How would this further action be justified? What is your appraisal of the situation?"

Galera stifled a belch. The very words were enough to cause

indigestion. Contact with his chief often made him think about the pleasures of retirement.

"We have first the death of Paradine. He is heavily sedated, he may have been murdered. Then the disappearance of Summers. Both men have been in Australia, have come from there recently. Then the disappearance of Rider. Are these all coincidences?"

"Possibly they are."

Galera shrugged his shoulders, a gesture of total weariness.

"If a crime has been committed in the province, that is our business. But is it certain that there has been any crime at all?"

"Santana thinks it very unlikely that Paradine would have been able to drive a car. He was too heavily sedated."

"But not impossible."

"Not impossible."

"And otherwise, what is the particular ground for suspecting a criminal offense?"

"Is it an accident that Rider is employing a convicted criminal?"

"He has been employed by others. And he has not been in prison for years. What are you suggesting?"

"And also an accident that Princeton or Paradine visits Rider?"

"What are you suggesting?"

"I am not sure. But the links are obvious."

Prieto tapped on his desk top. Everything on it shone—a silver inkstand, an oversize paper clip shaped like a claw, an ornate photograph frame with a picture of his wife inside. Galera's desk bore marks made by many hot coffee cups, and this morning he had found a fragment of fried fish mixed with his papers.

"What is it you wish to do?"

"Rider's wife is at the villa, and Paradine's brother. The woman perhaps knows where he is. She is a prostitute. Or perhaps she would simply like to be one." Galera waved a hand to indicate that he was not speaking quite literally.

"You have personal experience?" Prieto asked dryly.

"It is possible to tell such things."

"An enviable faculty. So what do you want?"

"I want to bring them in here, ask questions, keep them here. Not for long—two days, three perhaps. I shall soon learn what they know. Paradine wants to return to England, perhaps some of the others too."

"You would detain them here?"

"Until I am satisfied with their answers to my questions."

"What is there to ask questions about?"

"Félix, if we let these people go back to England, we shall regret it." He used Prieto's first name deliberately, knowing that the colonel disliked such familiarity, and knowing also that he would take it as a mark of Galera's seriousness about the affair. "Once we have let them return we shall never be able to question them. I *know* that there is a crime here."

"As you knew that Juan Sabre burned down his factory?"

The reference was to an incident a couple of years back, when Galera had been certain that a local businessman had arranged for the burning of his factory to collect the insurance money. The man, Juan Sabre, was an important member of the local Falange, and all charges against him had been dropped. Sabre had complained of the interrogation methods used, and Galera had been reprimanded.

"You know I was right."

"I know what happened. To me, what happens is right."

Galera hawked in his throat without actually spitting, and thought: What can you expect of a pompous bureaucrat sitting at a shiny desk?

"The answer is no."

"You mean, let them go?"

When Prieto used Galera's first name it meant that he was, with infinite patronage, correcting the errors of a rash subordinate. "What you do not understand, Manuel, is the trouble this can cause. Complaints from the British consul here, from the Embassy in Madrid. This Rider is an important man. Times have changed, things are not as they were twenty years ago. Tourism is important. Outside opinion is important. Do you know the first thing that will happen if I do as you ask? Questions from Madrid—why is this man or woman being detained, what do you suspect they have done?"

"They will have nothing to complain of. Our methods, too, are not those of twenty years ago."

"Nothing to complain of! Do you think that matters? In Spain a foreigner has only to be questioned for a couple of hours and he tells his consul he has been tortured. And it is believed, Manuel, it is believed. And then somebody in Madrid says, Who is this Galera asking so many questions, what do we know about him? Wasn't it a man of that name who pressed the case of the businessman, pressed a case against a good Falange member? A troublemaker, that Galera."

A fly buzzed on the windowpane. Galera thought about retirement. He would sit out in the courtyard of his little house and read again the philosophers he had studied in youth. How was it possible to be a good policeman in this country?

But Prieto was still speaking. "That is why I cannot agree, Manuel. You may be right, but you have no real proof, only guesswork."

"What do you want me to do, drop the whole thing?"

"But of course not. We put out a general notification about these two men who are missing. Perhaps Rider has simply left his wife, perhaps the other man has gone away to avoid payment of his bill, who knows?" I know, Galera thought, but he did not say so. "When we have *proof* that a crime has been committed on Spanish soil, then we pursue inquiries with all vigor."

Sunlight sparkled on Prieto's rimless glasses. Galera bowed his head.

12

On Wednesday Galera got a circulation from Interpol with more information about Summers and Paradine. It gave details of a dozen cases in which Summers had been suspected of involvement in violence not only for the gambling syndicate, but for other employers. A man named Shepherd had been shot to death in a Melbourne street a week before he was due to give evidence in a corruption case concerning a city councillor; a dealer in secondhand goods known as Buffalo Bernie had been stabbed to death in Sydney; just outside Sydney a woman secretary named Joan Swan had been knocked down and killed by a hit-and-run driver. There was one further piece of news about Paradine that linked the two men. The firm Joan Swan worked for had been Austro-Asian Products.

Galera pointed out the link to Prieto, who was not impressed. He could not speak to the English party, even if he had wanted to do so, because they had flown back to London on the previous day.

PART THREE | Investigations

1

Roger Rider was a figure of sufficient importance for his disappearance to make newspaper headlines for a couple of days. Eric Coope read about it in the *Daily Telegraph*, and felt that he ought to report the little job he had carried out for Rider to the police. On the other hand, the job didn't seem much to report, and he was afraid that they might laugh at him. Finally, he rang up a sergeant with whom he was on drinking terms, and the sergeant reported the matter at his station. Not long after that Coope found himself in an office at New Scotland Yard, telling the story to a ruddy-cheeked, curly-haired man in plain clothes. The man, who had introduced himself as Sergeant Maitland, did not laugh.

"What stuck in my mind was that once he'd found out who the other man was, he didn't want to go on with it. That's unusual. I mean, if you know your wife's been playing around with somebody, it's only human nature to want the evidence, isn't it?"

"Right you are." Maitland was biting a pencil end.

"I mean, you'd expect him to want to do something about it."

"How do you know he didn't? He may have gone home straightaway and beaten hell out of his wife."

Coope was taken aback. "Oh, I don't think— I mean, he didn't strike me as that kind of man."

"You'd be surprised by what kind of man we all are. Or, since you're in the private inquiry business, perhaps you wouldn't. Anyway, Rider never came back to you, just paid your account and that was it?"

"That's correct. Except that he paid generously, more than my bill."

"Unusual again."

"Very." Wistfully, in the hope of catching some romantic crumb dropped from the well-laden table of real criminal work, Coope said, "You're interested in his disappearance, then?"

"We're interested in all disappearances. Many thanks, Mr. Coope, you've been very helpful."

2

Grilled chops, potatoes baked in the oven, frozen broccoli, then crumbly Stilton. The pleasures of being back in England, and in the little flat, were simple but real. And not the least of them was that of seeing Jerry Maitland on the other side of the table, and being able to read throughout the meal. James read about the Brink's Garage robbery in Boston, meticulously planned and carried out by clever professionals who got clean away with a million and a quarter dollars, only to be betrayed by an informer. Had any work of fiction matched the thoroughness with which these thieves had gone about their job, even using a dry run to remove the locks from the doors, making new keys for them, and then refitting the locks before they left? Jerry had the *Evening Standard* propped up before him. When they had finished eating he pushed it aside, and took from his pocket the letters James had written from Spain. Two sheets of foolscap and a pencil appeared from nowhere. "Now," he said. "Let's have it."

"You look very official, Jerry. Are you going to grill me?"

"When I grill you, boy, you'll feel the heat."

"You're not going to tell me anything I say may be used in evidence?"

"The word isn't 'used,' it's 'given.' " He tapped the letters with his pencil. "But when I said I wanted to know about Rider, it wasn't a joke then and it's dead serious now. I want everything that happened after you wrote these letters—what you saw, thought, anything you can remember. So let's have it."

"All right." James told him everything, and ended by producing the sheet of paper he had found in Summers' room.

Jerry frowned over it. "You're sure this is your uncle's writing? Yes, I see you are." He clipped the letter to the foolscap sheets. "And you really think he was referring to Summers and this Miss Swan in the game you played?"

"I don't think there's any doubt. Jerry, you can't leave it at that without telling me a bit of what it's about, not after all my hard labor."

"Let's wash up these things." He talked while he washed and James dried. "I can't tell you much. I've been following a tip, but what happened in Spain is a surprise to me. I don't know anything about your uncle, or about Summers." He washed a glass more thoroughly than he need have done. "One more thing, and for God's sake don't say I told you. Rider knew about your father's affair with his wife, the green-eyed beauty. He'd put a private detective onto Mrs. Rider, and the man had seen your father going into Rider's flat."

"That's all over. She said that, and he says so too."

"I daresay, but is it true? Did Rider get your father out to Spain to have some kind of showdown? And if they had a showdown and Rider told your father not to see his wife again, what would have happened?"

"I told you, nothing happened. It's finished."

Jerry dried his hands, put one of them on James's shoulder. "I know you told me. But I can't take it on your say-so, you see that?"

3

On the following morning Jerry talked to Feathers, who heard him without notable enthusiasm and asked what he wanted to do.

"Go and see Stephenson, the managing director of BMS. Ask him a few questions. See the prospective widow. Tell the Spanish police about this letter in Summers' room. Run our own check on Hubert Paradine and Summers through Interpol. Ask the Australian police for anything they can give us on these two firms, Austro-Asian Products and Intertrade. Go and see Geoffrey Paradine—that's the father of the man I share a flat with."

"You must like making work."

"I don't get you."

"Most of this is none of our bloody business. Take this report from the inquiry agent. If Mrs. Rider was getting a bit on the side, what's it to do with us? Come to that, what's any of it to do with us? This Paradine dies in Spain, two other buggers disappear there. All right, let the bloody Spaniards pull their fingers out and look for them. They've already asked us a pile of questions, by the way. Lawton was on to me this morning. Why should we split a gut because some silly little girl told you stories out of school about a firm she was probably sacked from? How did you find her, by the way?"

"At a party. She found me. Afterward we improved our acquaintance." Maitland grinned, then said gloomily, "But, Super, do you really mean—"

"I'm just pointing out that you're probably wasting time, you randy young devil. We're the Fraud Squad, and you haven't shown me any fraud yet."

"You want me to drop it?"

"No, you do what you said, only don't spend too much time on it, that's all."

"Just one thing." He knew that Feathers liked him, knew too that although the old man was devoted to his wife and family he still liked chatting up an attractive bird. "Mrs. Rider. I don't think I ought to trust myself with her. Why don't you take her on yourself? I mean, it sounds as though she goes for older men."

Feathers called him a cheeky young bastard, then laughed and agreed. It had occurred to him that if there was by chance anything in the affair, it might not be a bad idea for him to be involved at this stage.

4

Alastair Stephenson was what the name had led Maitland to expect. He wore a plain brown suit that buttoned up almost to the neck, a plain shirt and a gaily patterned yet somehow still discreet tie. His hair was long, but not obtrusively so. He used the vowel sounds of the upper class, but did so with an air of listening to the sounds himself and finding them slightly amusing. His head was thin, like his body, and he had a languid manner that Maitland thought might be misleading. *Who's Who* had told the sergeant that Stephenson had been educated at one of the right schools and one of the right universities, and that he had taken a First Class in Hon. Mods, whatever that might be. He was a chartered accountant, had a lot of directorships and had become Managing Director of BMS three years earlier. In a way, he represented something Maitland would have liked to be, and the sergeant's manner was correspondingly brusque. Stephenson confirmed that they had heard nothing from Rider. Was he concerned?

"He's our Chairman. Naturally, everybody here is concerned."

"He's been away now nearly a week. You had no idea that anything like this might happen? It came as a total surprise?"

"Anything like what, sergeant? Obviously, I had no idea that he was going to disappear. That can hardly be what you mean."

"I'll put it plainer. Was there any trouble inside the firm? Did he have any financial problems?"

"Not to my knowledge. Of course, I don't know about any personal problems."

"BMS shares have dropped since he disappeared."

Stephenson paused in the act of lighting a long-tipped cigarette, then said casually, "They'll rise again."

"What's his holding in the firm?" When Stephenson did not reply, he said, "I can easily find out."

"Precisely. Because of that, I wondered why you should ask. His holding is rather under twenty percent. Mine is roughly half of that. We are a public company, of course. What's behind these questions, sergeant?"

Let's try and give the smug bastard a jolt, Maitland thought. "Either there's been some attack on Mr. Rider or he vanished willingly. If it was the first, then it's up to the Spanish police, but if he intended to disappear, it might be because he was in financial trouble. And he wasn't?"

"I repeat, not to my knowledge."

"He handled part of the Foreign Sales Department himself, I believe. The crude-drugs section, right?" With the pleasure of a boxer who has at last got through a difficult opponent's guard, he saw Stephenson's eyes flicker.

"Correct."

"Is the head of Foreign Sales—that's Mr. Geoffrey Paradine— around? Can I have a word with him?"

For the first time Stephenson's words came sharply. "Mr. Paradine is still on leave. His future in the firm is not settled. And in any case, before you talk to him or to anybody else, I shall want to know the reason for these questions. I'm not prepared to have a policeman going round the office asking questions which are certain to upset people here, unless there's some very good reason. Do I make myself clear?"

"Quite clear. How about his personal life? Any problems there?"

"I know very little about Roger's personal life." Stephenson's manner had become increasingly glacial. How to turn the frozen mitt into a complete cold shoulder, Maitland thought. He nibbled at his pencil.

"You mean you never visited his house, and he hasn't been to yours? If not, either you disliked each other or you can't have done much entertaining."

"That was an unnecessary remark." Stephenson paused again, and Maitland thought, I've gone too far, he's dried up for good. But he was wrong. "My wife and I went down two or three times to Pevering Manor. Roger and his wife dined with us more than once. But that doesn't qualify me to talk about his private life. In fact, sergeant, I'm not going to say anything more to you at all. And if a superior of yours asks me why not, I shall tell him that I didn't like either your questions or the way you put them." He uncoiled from behind the desk, a thin tall man with a head like a hawk's.

At least I never called the bastard *sir*, Maitland thought with pleasure as he made a not particularly dignified exit.

5

Feathers didn't like the very modern furniture or the odd pictures on the walls, but he was pleasantly impressed by Amanda. She wore a plain dark dress without ornament, her manner was quiet, she didn't look in the least like the figure in young Paradine's letter. He had expected something more sultry and more opulent. He accepted a glass of whisky, noting appreciatively that it was a malt, sat in a chair like an uncoiling spring and listened to what she had to say.

"I don't have any idea at all what's happened, superintendent, absolutely no idea. Every time the telephone rings I think it may be Roger. One thing I'm sure of: I'm not saying ours was an ideal marriage or anything like that, but he'd never have walked out on me."

"Then something must have happened to him."

"I didn't think so at first, but now I'm afraid it has. He wouldn't have gone off without being in touch with me. I tell you, superintendent, I'm afraid he's dead." She said it in a voice quite lacking in obvious emotion, and then took a quick gulp at her glass. She too was drinking whisky. "Is that what you think?"

"Did he have any enemies you know of, either in business or personal enemies?"

"I didn't know much about his business, though of course I've met some of the directors at dinner parties and cocktail parties. But enemies, I just don't know. Personal enemies—well, not so far as I know. Come to think of it, how many people do have personal enemies, people who'd want to do them harm?"

"Did he say anything to you about Hubert Paradine?"

"He said he wasn't much like Geoff, that's all. You know, Roger and Geoff are old friends. Otherwise nothing. Why should he?"

This response to a question by asking another question in reply was annoying Feathers.

"If your marriage was a happy one, why did your husband employ a private detective to check on your movements?"

Whatever reaction he had expected, it was not the smile he got. "What, again? When was this, superintendent?"

He noted that she had again adroitly avoided answering him by asking another question. "What was the previous occasion, Mrs. Rider?"

"Oh, two years ago, I suppose. I was having an affair with a young TV actor named Basil Deeley, and Roger got absurdly jealous. By the time his bloodhound had reported back, I'd got bored. The whole thing was over."

"Have you often had affairs?"

She said with composure, "It depends what you call often. We've been married five years and I've had four—no, five, I suppose you might say if you include a very quick one. I shouldn't say that was many, would you?"

The solid fleshiness of Feathers' own wife always made him think of steak-and-kidney pudding when she was undressed, but he felt a stirring of indignation at Amanda's calmness. "What was your husband's attitude? You say he was jealous."

"Oh, he was. He used to get upset, very. But it never lasted. The affairs didn't, either. You still haven't told me when he was having me followed."

"In early July. You were having an affair then?"

She nodded. "I'll tell you something funny, though. He never mentioned it to me, and he'd always said something about the others. So naturally I supposed he didn't know. This is a shock."

You look about as shocked as the Mona Lisa, the superintendent thought, and wondered if this was the time to disclose that he knew the name of her last lover. Her next words saved him the trouble.

"But then I suppose it was a shock to him too. I mean, finding out that it was Geoffrey."

"Geoffrey Paradine?"

"You knew that, didn't you?" she said as calmly as though she were saying that he had a watch and knew the time.

"Paradine was—is—your husband's oldest friend." Feathers' feelings had changed. He found himself disliking this woman more every moment, and what annoyed him most was her complete composure. He had the feeling that if he accused her of murdering her husband, cutting his body into little cubes and then stewing and eating them, she would consider the suggestion and then say: *He would have been too tough.* "Is that why you chose him?" he asked, and she did consider the question, sipping delicately at the last drops in her glass.

"Perhaps." She asked if he would like some more whisky, and smiled when he refused. "Are you thinking 'I'm not going to drink with her, she might put arsenic in the whisky'? I'm sorry if you don't like my frankness. I'm afraid that in the sense you use the word, I've got no morals."

"I quite agree." He knew that he should not have said that. Her smile, insulting and confiding, showed that she knew it too.

"These things are not as important as you think them. Not to me, nor to Roger, in spite of his jealousy. He knew what I'm like, and he accepted it. For me Geoffrey Paradine was something new. Inhibited but rather creative, and that was interesting. And, as you say, the attraction was partly that he was Roger's oldest friend." She dropped suddenly into Cockney. "Don't look at me in that tone of voice, super, you make me go all of a shiver."

"Anybody who could make you shiver would deserve a medal."

"Don't be so uptight. I thought policemen were meant to understand human nature. Well, when human nature—that is, *my* nature—says to me, going to bed with that man would be fun or interesting, I go to bed with him if I can. I don't get too many refusals. And when I decide that the thing's finished, then it's finished. It hardly ever lasts long with me."

"And Geoffrey Paradine is finished."

"Yes. I told him so in Spain. We hadn't met before then for a little while."

"And how did he take his dismissal?"

She shrugged.

"What does that mean?"

"He was upset. But he'll get over it."

"Did it occur to you that this was dangerous, having an affair with your husband's best friend, that he might be very angry?"

"I've told you, Roger understands me."

"Who arranged this holiday in Spain?"

"It was Roger's idea, but actually I suggested that he should ask Geoff. I thought it might be fun, but it wasn't. He was just a bore."

"So the whole holiday was boring," he said ironically.

She treated the question seriously. "It would have been if it had gone on. I don't think I could have endured a month of it. Geoffrey's son James is madly attractive to look at, but I think he's probably queer."

Feathers looked at her, a neat figure in her bubble chair, at home among the incomprehensible paintings, the furniture with its unlikely shapes. You're getting past it, he thought, you don't understand what makes these people tick. As though she had guessed his thoughts, she said, "This doesn't make sense to you, does it? For me, when you begin an affair you do it because you both know what you're doing, and when one of you feels it's over, you just draw a line."

"And go on to the next?" She made a dismissive gesture, as though he were a persistent but harmless fly. He felt the stirrings of anger again. "Did Paradine know what he was doing? It doesn't sound like it to me."

"Why don't you ask him?"

6

It was a week later, after he had answers to his inquiries in Australia and had answered queries from the Spanish police that came through Lawton, that Maitland saw Geoffrey Paradine in the small living room at Malbite Street. He introduced himself, they talked about James, he looked at pictures showing school groups, and then he got down to asking questions, first of all about the extent of Rider's interest in Foreign Sales. Paradine seemed bewildered.

"He takes an interest, yes. Or should I say took? I don't know what more I can say."

"What aspects of them did he deal with personally?"

"He takes a general interest. But, yes, I suppose you mean the crude-drugs section, he always dealt with that."

Maitland nibbled his pencil. "Mr. Paradine, suppose he had wanted to put certain items through without your knowledge.

Would that have been possible?"

"I expect so. But why should he want to do that?"

"Do you know who handled the distribution of your products in Australia?"

"I think so, yes. There was one firm called Austro-Asian Products, and another called— I can't remember."

"Intertrade."

"That's right." He beamed. "I think we shipped out to Austro-Asian, and then Intertrade handled the selling end. It's a very important market. They sell all over the Far East."

"Do you know who ran Intertrade out in Sydney?"

"No, I know nothing about it, I'm afraid."

Would it have been possible to get anybody dimmer to handle a department? Maitland wondered. "Your brother, Hubert Paradine."

Either Geoffrey Paradine was ignorant of this or he was a remarkable actor. He goggled at the sergeant with his mouth open.

"He'd been running it for three years. Do you know of a woman named Swan, Joan Swan, who worked for Austro-Asian? She was a secretary. She died in a car accident, killed by a hit-and-run driver. Never heard of her? Very well. We asked the Sydney police to talk to somebody at Austro-Asian, but they had no luck. The offices are closed. The Intertrade office is closed too."

Paradine repeated incredulously, "Hubert worked for BMS. I can hardly believe it."

"I agree. I should have thought you'd be certain to know."

Paradine shook his head like a man in shock.

"How direct were your own dealings with Austro-Asian and Intertrade?"

"I had no dealings with them, as you call it. The department sent out invoices and that kind of thing, of course, but really Roger handled all that." He stared at Maitland. "*Roger* must have known that Hubert was working for BMS."

"Just what I was coming to. Were there any signs that they knew each other?"

"I didn't notice any. But I wasn't looking for them."

"There was a game you played in which your brother mentioned 'summer' and 'swan.' James thinks he was referring deliberately to a man named Summers who's disappeared, and to this woman Joan Swan."

"It may be. I really didn't notice."

Jerry couldn't refrain from saying, "You don't notice much, do you?"

"I'm afraid I don't. And I was never good at the job. It was only through Roger that I kept it. When I was in Spain I decided to send in my resignation. Roger was going to move me to another department, but I should have been just as bad anywhere else." In a matter-of-fact way he said, "I really wasn't cut out for business, I'm afraid."

"All this wouldn't be connected with your relationship with Mrs. Rider, would it? We know about that."

Geoffrey Paradine stared at him. "Roger didn't know."

"Indeed he did, sir."

"But that's extraordinary! He never said anything to me."

"He'd had his wife followed. You'd been seen entering and leaving their flat. Rider knew about the whole thing." Jerry jabbed a finger at Paradine. "Suppose that was why he'd asked you out to Spain. And then out there he had a showdown with you, right? Perhaps that day you were out in a boat together. Then afterward you killed him. Isn't that the way it happened?"

Geoffrey shook his head. He looked like a stricken rabbit. "Oh, no, no, no. Roger never said a word to me, you have to believe that."

Jerry Maitland did not much care for sessions like this, but he plugged on for another twenty minutes without result. Later he discussed the visit with Feathers, who still considered the whole thing a waste of time. No doubt some fiddle had been going on in Australia, whether or not Geoffrey Paradine knew about it, but the Fraud Squad was concerned with fraud in Britain. There was, God knew, enough of it around, and he had his own hands full with an attempt to disentangle the interlocking company structures arranged by the presiding genius of a vehicle-insurance group. It would be nice if they had time and people to spare for looking into fraud in Australia, but they hadn't.

"It's at times like that that I feel like packing it in and taking that job out in South America." Maitland had told the superintendent a couple of months earlier about the job offered him in Buenos Aires as the chief security officer of a large corporation.

"You wouldn't like it, Jerry. All those señoritas would be too much for you."

"What gets up my nose is the thought that Rider's just skipped out, collected the couple of million he's salted away somewhere and got out to B.A. before me."

"You don't have any real evidence."

"No."

"So for the moment we have to put it in the pending file. If there's any break in the case, and if it involves fraud, we've done our homework. Agreed?"

Jerry Maitland sighed. "I suppose so."

7

James was reading a book called *Great American Swindles* when the telephone rang. A voice said, "Sheila."

"Sheila who?"

"Sheila Rider—how many Sheilas do you know? Look, it's about my father. He hasn't come back, and nobody seems even to be doing anything about it. I've just been to see my awful stepmother, and she says there's nothing to do but wait." A pause. "Are you there? Do I sound hysterical?"

"No, just dogmatic as usual."

"You share this flat with your policeman boyfriend, don't you?"

"He's not my boyfriend."

"All right, but he must know something about it. I've been to Scotland Yard, and they just say I'll hear from the Spanish police when they have some news. It isn't good enough. I'm not going to leave it at that. Can't your friend find out something?"

"Possibly. I'll see what I can do." On impulse he invited her to come and watch Chelsea on Saturday. He was slightly disturbed by the alacrity with which she accepted.

Five minutes later the key turned in the lock, and Jerry came in. James told him what Sheila had said.

"I don't know who she spoke to, but that's right. Whatever happened happened in Spain, so it's the job of the old Espaniolas to investigate it. Fraud Squad's too busy, can't spare the time. That's official, from the horse's mouth. Or the horse's arse." He flung down his document case. "And investigating is probably what the Dons are doing at this moment. There's a development. A body's been washed ashore near where you were staying, and it looks as though it may be Rider."

8

The break in the case came on a day in October nearly five weeks after Rider's disappearance.

The body was seen in the water about two kilometers away from Valeta by a fisherman who hooked it, towed it ashore and reported his discovery to the Guardia Civil. In due course it was examined by Dr. Santana, and his report came onto Galera's desk. The body was that of a bulky well-preserved man between forty-five and fifty-five years old. This fitted Rider, but it also fitted Summers. A few sodden rags of clothing adhered to it, but they gave no clue to identity. The body itself was unrecognizable, · because of decomposition and also because much of it had been thoroughly eaten by fish. Galera talked to Santana, and said that it might be the missing Englishman, the important one. Could they bring his wife over to make an identification?

"No use. Quite unrecognizable."

"Fingerprints?"

"They don't exist."

"Scars? Old operations?"

Santana grunted. "Haven't found anything important. Don't think there is anything. When the body tissue's gone—" Santana was a professional pessimist.

"The teeth?"

"Yes, the teeth are a possibility. You want me to have a dental chart prepared?"

"The idea is to make an identification," Galera said, and regretted the sarcasm. As a softening touch he added, "Many thanks."

"Don't mention it."

"Is there anything else that might be useful?"

"One thing. Around the right wrist was a piece of rope, and on the left a mark as if another piece had been attached. There were similar marks on the legs, though no sign of a rope."

"You mean the body may have been tied to a heavy weight to keep it down?"

"Something like that. Perhaps the lab can help."

But the help given by the laboratory was minimal. Galera could not help feeling that things would have been different in Britain. The bits of clothing were analyzed. They were not of Spanish manufacture, and were either English or American. The rope was of a kind available anywhere. It had not been frayed, but appeared to have been deliberately cut, and embedded in it were flecks of rusty metal. So far and no further went the laboratory information.

Galera thought about it. The fact that there were marks on hands and legs strongly suggested a weight keeping down the body in the water, the deliberate cutting of the rope that somebody wanted the body to be found, and perhaps found round about this particular time. Perhaps the rope-cutter had waited until the corpse was unrecognizable. Galera was pleased by this deduction. It led him to the Villa Victoria.

He found María there, and José the gardener, but not Rodríguez. A frightened María (police in uniform, like the Guardia Civil or the Policía Armada, make Spaniards nervous, but police in plain clothes terrify them) said that he had left five days ago. Quite suddenly he had packed his things and gone, without a word to her. An examination of his room showed that he had made a clean sweep of everything in it. María had no idea why he had left. Their salary was still being paid, so that could not be the reason. Galera questioned her sharply, and decided that she knew no more than she had told him. He saw the motorboats. Had Rodríguez used them a lot, he asked. Perhaps he had been a fisherman? Yes, he had used them for fishing. Galera had himself taken out in a boat by José, and carefully examined the buoys. He found one on which there might have been rope marks. The buoy was rusty under the water surface, and he was able to get a few fragments of the rust into a waterproof bag.

Back at the office, he sent the fragments for comparison with those embedded in the rope, and put out a notice for the arrest of Rodríguez Orantes wherever he might be found. He went home that evening feeling pleased with himself. His own María found him expansive as he told her that he had talked to another María that day who had been terrified of him. She giggled as she unstrapped the shoulder holster in which he kept his revolver.

"She did not know you as I know you."

"Be careful, woman. A Jefe de Servicio commands respect." She tickled him. He squirmed with laughter. When she had stopped he pulled her onto his knees. "You remember the puzzle I told you of, the classical puzzle of the disappearances? A body has been found. Which of them is it, the businessman Rider or the other? What has Rodríguez to do with it? Did Rider engage him because he was a criminal? Did Rodríguez dispose of the body?"

"I thought the colonel said that time was not to be wasted—"

"That was before this body had been found. In any case, our stupid little colonel is on leave. I, Manuel Galera, am in charge. There is a case to be solved and I shall solve it. If it goes well it may make me as famous as Maigret."

"I thought he was a man in a book."

The remark reminded him that women were very well in their place, which was on their backs in bed, but that it was impossible to hold an intelligent conversation with them. He turned María over, gave her buttocks one powerful slap and said, "Out to where you belong, the kitchen. I am hungry. If the Jefe de Servicio's meal is not ready in half an hour—" He tapped the leather belt he wore. She put her hands together in mock supplication.

On the following afternoon his exhilaration increased when the laboratory reported that the rust fragments embedded in the rope and those scraped off the buoy were identical. Was this not a brilliant piece of inspirational thinking? He felt the need of an audience, and called in Sergeant Gómez. The sergeant was beetle-browed and blue-jowled, short and thick. He listened in silence to Galera's exposition.

"You see what this means, Gómez? This man was killed, then tied to the buoy, with his body roped to it by the hands, weights roped to the feet. He is kept there for five weeks. Then the rope is cut, the body rises. Somebody wishes it to be discovered. If we ask who cut the rope, the answer is Rodríguez, but if we ask *why*, then what is the answer?"

Gómez grunted. His voice was a growl produced from somewhere in his stomach. "Rodríguez."

"Rodríguez what?"

"He is cheating the Englishman Rider. They ask to be cheated, the English. The cheat is discovered, Rodríguez kills him, ties the body. When it comes loose he knows it is time to go."

Galera frowned. It was not at all his intention that Gómez should step outside his role of listener. "The body did not come loose, it was cut away. Why would Rodríguez have done that?"

"Who knows?"

"Who knows? *We* shall know when Rodríguez is brought in."

126

Without change of expression the sergeant placed a piece of paper on the desk. As he did so his jacket opened to reveal the revolver tucked into his trousers. Galera frowned again to show his displeasure at the weapon so openly displayed, then read the message. It was from Madrid, and said that Rodríguez Orantes had taken a plane to London nearly forty-eight hours earlier. His passport had been made out in the name of Martínez. The identification was certain. The man had signed a customs form, and the prints made on it by Martínez corresponded with the file prints of Rodríguez.

Galera hid his annoyance. He had envisaged the interrogation of Rodríguez, the revelations made by him which led into further mysteries involving Rider and the mysterious Summers. He saw himself flying to England, conferences at New Scotland Yard, the villain trapped in an East End warehouse. He knew that such imaginative flights were taking him too far. In fact he would ask for extradition of the man they wanted to put on trial, and if the man was British they would have to make out a strong case before they got him. He came back to reality, and Gómez's little black eyes watching him. Gómez was a powerful irritant. Galera pressed down a switch, and said to his secretary, "Put in a call to London. Inspector Lawton at New Scotland Yard."

The sergeant looked about to spit. "What will the colonel say?"

"The colonel is on leave." In his absence Galera indulged one of his daydreams—the telephone call to Scotland Yard, the cooperation asked for and enthusiastically given, the personal touch and not a dreary sending of cables. When he got through, Lawton was just as friendly as he had expected. His heart warmed toward the English.

9

"Sit down, sergeant."

Maitland sat a little nervously in the chair. He felt that the dentist might tell him to put his head back and open wide, then get to work with a drill. In fact the dentist said apologetically, "Sorry to put you in the hot seat, but we don't have a chair for visitors."

The dentist's name was Charles Hoskins, and, like other fashionable dentists, he occupied part of a house in Wimpole Street. He was a self-assured smiling man in his early thirties. Amanda Rider had given his name on the telephone.

"I've got his chart here. He has very good teeth, or perhaps I should say had." Hoskins flashed his smile at Maitland. Hoskins' own teeth were magnificent.

"The details came from Spain by telegram. I'm afraid we don't have a chart, though of course we can get one if you need it." Maitland handed over the telegram.

Hoskins studied it, looked up with his smile. "This will take a minute or two. The Spaniards have a different notation system from ours." After just two minutes he looked up again and nodded.

"They're the same?"

"Yes. You see it says here on the telegram '1+ pivot crown.' The plus sign in that notation means the middle of the upper jaw and 1+ is the first tooth from the middle to the right side. You can see it on our chart, marked as crowned. Then 4+ is missing, and it's shown as missing on the chart. There's another crown in the upper jaw—here it is on the chart—and a small gold inlay in the lower jaw, that's the one marked with a minus sign on the telegram. It's all identical."

Maitland took the chart and looked at it. "I'd like to take this away. We'll have it copied and return it to you."

"By all means."

"You say Rider had pretty good teeth. When was the last time he came to you?"

"He didn't come to me personally. He was my partner's patient—that's Norman Smith. Norman retired just over a year ago. He lives somewhere near Menton now, I believe. Strictly speaking, Rider ought to have been along to see me since Norman's retirement, but in practice people often ignore reminders until they get twinges. Unless you get in touch with Norman, I'm afraid you can't talk to anybody who actually dealt with Rider's teeth—"

Maitland protested that the chart was all they needed, but Hoskins held up a hand. His smile was firmly in place.

"I was going on to say, but we can have a look at the record card on which Norman will have recorded Rider's visits and the dates on which work was done." He pressed a buzzer and a pale washed-out blonde appeared. "Miss Shaw, would you get me Mr. Smith's card on Mr. Rider, Roger Rider." During her five minutes' absence Hoskins made conversation about the excitement of catching criminals. Jerry said that it was mostly paperwork.

When Miss Shaw came back she was a little paler. She said that they hadn't got the card. Hoskins' smile vanished. She explained.

"After Mr. Smith retired, any of his patients who didn't come back after we sent two reminders, we put their cards on one side. I asked Mrs. Howard and she said, I thought she said, it was all right to get rid of them because they probably weren't coming back. Mr. Rider's card was one of those."

"The cards were to be destroyed only when it was certain that a client had changed to another dentist." Miss Shaw muttered something inaudible, and was dismissed. "Inefficiency everywhere," Hoskins said, and put his smile back into place.

Maitland said it didn't matter, the dental chart was the vital thing. They sent the information through to Major Galera, and he talked the situation over with Feathers.

"That's it, then," the superintendent said. "Whatever happened happened in Spain. For us it's finished." Maitland's bullet head was bent down over his desk. "You don't like it?"

"No."

"Then you can do the other thing. If there was a fraud going on, Rider must have been in it. He was our lead. Now he's dead and we've got no lead at all. You must see I'm making sense, Jerry."

"Are you telling me, with what we've found out, that something somewhere doesn't stink? Out in Australia, and in Spain too?"

"It's not just that I'm looking for an easy life before retirement."

"No." The statement was not quite a question.

"I'll pretend I didn't hear the way you said that." Feathers liked Jerry Maitland and was prepared to take a bit of lip from him, but there was a limit. "I don't know what we're arguing about. The dental chart says it loud and clear, Rider's dead. It looks like he was murdered, and if the Spaniards want any help from us apart from laying hands on this Orantes, they'll ask for it. Apart from that, we leave it. We've got other things to do. Okay?"

"Okay." Feathers looked at his watch. "They're open. Come on and I'll buy you a jar."

Over the beer Maitland said, "I tell you one thing. The next time anyone offers me a job out of England at four times what I get here, I shan't think twice before saying yes."

"Leave London's finest? You must be joking." But he could not be sure that Maitland was.

To James that evening Jerry explained some of the frustrations of being a policeman in these particular circumstances, while they ate a bacon, eggs and chips, and drank Tuborg beer.

"The trouble with a case like this is, it doesn't belong to anybody. Or it belongs to everybody. There's nothing in it for us, we're the Fraud Squad, and as far as the CID's concerned it's all something that happened in Spain. You could put the evidence we've got of something criminal happening here on a new halfpenny, and there'd still be room round the edges. I'm telling you all this in confidence, you sod, remember that."

"I've got the recorder running, and I'll send the tape up to the Yard tomorrow." Jerry's head jerked back. "Sorry, bad joke. But Rider's been murdered, surely that must count for something?"

"Don't make any more jokes like that, my heart won't stand

them. I may want to leave the Yard, but not neck first." He drained his beer, looked at his watch. "I've got to meet a snout in a pub in an hour. But the point about Rider that Feathers keeps hammering is that it all took place in Spain, the good old refrain. I've told you before, cock, it's only if a crime has been committed on our own sacred soil that we really get into gear."

"Bloody stupid. We've got time for a game before you go off to meet your snout."

They played, and Jerry lost. He always kept the score, and looking at his friend's head bent over the paper, James felt that familiar tide of tenderness sweeping up. Perhaps Sheila was right and he ought to say, "I can't stand this, either we do something about it or I shall have to leave." But was that really what he wanted? While he was brooding on this, Jerry added the scores.

"Four hundred points behind. It must be love I'm lucky at. I'll tell you something. When I've seen this disgusting little snout, I'm going to have myself a skinful and pick up a dolly and screw her till her thread's worn out. So if you come barging in my room, you know what you'll find."

For the rest of the evening James read about American crime. He read about Billie Sol Estes, whose liquid-fertilizer empire was founded on a fiddle, and Tony de Angelis, who made a corner in what proved to be non-existent soybean oil, and Philip Musica, who had special Bradstreet typewriters made to type favorable reports on his non-existent corporations. He was still up when Jerry returned after midnight, slightly drunk, alone and in a bad temper.

"Lose at cards, not allowed to catch villains and now I can't even catch birds. Took one out to dinner, and afterward what do you think she said? Her mother would be waiting up because it was past her bedtime. I tell you, cock, I'm losing my touch. Do you know what I've a good mind to do? Ask if they've kept that job in Buenos Aires open. They said there was a place for me any time."

James took Sheila to the Great American Disaster in the Fulham Road, less than ten minutes' walk from the Chelsea ground. They ate hamburgers, drank milk shakes, tried to talk under a powerful barrage of noise from a jukebox and the other customers. In the end they abandoned the attempt. He sat looking a little gloomily at his companion, who had kitted herself out in what she obviously thought the appropriate style for a Chelsea supporter, in dark-blue jersey and slacks, with a large blue-and-white scarf wound round her neck and a blue cap with a white peak.

"Where's your rattle?"

"What?"

"Never mind."

"You're supposed to support Chelsea, but you don't wear anything in their colors. You've even got a red tie."

He started to say that his support was too deeply emotional to need expression in symbols, but gave up when it was plain that she could not hear. When they came out a thin rain was falling. They trudged along the road with thousands of others, a one-way traffic.

"I thought you were an intellectual," she said. "I'm surprised at you liking something like this. Intellect having a rest?"

"On the contrary, watching football stimulates the intellect. I was sorry about your father being found. Sorry for you, I mean."

"Thanks. But do you know, I didn't feel anything at all. I suppose there's no special reason why I should. I'd hardly seen him for years. Did you speak to your policeman?"

"Yes."

"Is it absolutely certain?"

"Apparently the dental identification is positive, though there's one slightly odd thing." He told her about the dental card having been destroyed. "You can't even call it odd, just that the record card would have been a final check, that's all."

"It is odd, though." She nodded emphatically, and the peaked cap fell off. James picked it up before an oncoming red-and-white Arsenal supporter could tread on it. She replaced it at an angle. "Very odd. I'll tell you something. About two months ago I was walking down Holborn and my father came out of a café with a woman. It was a cheap café, not his kind of place at all. He was obviously embarrassed when he saw me, but he stopped—he had to, really, hadn't he?—and as the woman walked away he called out to her that he'd be in touch. I asked him who it was, and he said his dental receptionist, he'd met her in there by accident, and seeing her had reminded him that he ought to make an appointment. I asked what he was doing in a place like that, and he said he liked to remind himself of the way the other half lived. Then afterward on the phone he told me it was his mistress, which was a joke. I meant to ask him about it in Spain, but I never did."

"What was the woman like?"

"Pale and mousy, not very old. I didn't pay her too much attention. Do you know what this dental receptionist looks like?"

They were inside the ground by now, and queuing to pass through the turnstiles. He spoke to the back of her neck. "Jerry didn't say. But it might be worth trying to find out."

Inside, he bought programs. The fans were singing the Chelsea song, with a dirge-like beat:

> "Blue is the color, football is the game.
> Blue is the color, Chelsea is the name."

She gave a smothered laugh.

"What's funny?"

"Just you saying football stimulates the intellect."

"A footballer's intellect is in his feet."

"Is that so? Very dirty here, isn't it? I thought it would be more like Wimbledon tennis."

"I don't know where you were brought up. Football's the game the workers go to watch."

"I didn't know," she said meekly. "And I'm sorry if I've got the wrong clothes on. I did try to dress for the occasion."

"You succeeded. Only too well."

"How was I to know what the well-dressed fan looks like?"

"Doesn't matter."

They were walking under a covered section behind a stand. A row of policemen stood watching the fans who filed past them. At one side half a dozen boys wearing bovver boots had been stopped, and were arguing resignedly with a policeman. "They try to keep Chelsea and the other supporters at different ends of the ground in case of trouble."

"Will there be trouble?"

"I shouldn't think so, but with Arsenal, a London derby, it's always on the cards." As they went up the steps to the stand they heard a roar like the baying of fifty thousand dogs. "That's the players coming out."

From seats high up they looked down on red and blue framed in green. Puppet figures jumped up and down, kicked out legs, flung arms high, did little sprints. The referee dashed onto the field, a white ball under his arm, summoned the captains with a whistle. The players lined up, Chelsea's Hudson tapped the ball to Garland, who passed it back to Hollins. The game had begun.

Sheila watched the first five minutes in fascination. "It's like a ballet, isn't it, all that heading of the ball? So pretty."

James was leaning forward, watching intently. He gave her a brief half-smile, then turned back again. The red shirts of Arsenal surged up the field. The whistle blew, play stopped.

"What happened then?"

"Foul by Harris on Armstrong. Free kick."

From the kick, one of the blues booted it upfield to where a solitary blue player waited. He got the ball. Sheila was astonished to hear James shout, "Bloody well get onside, you lazy bugger!" The blue player made no attempt to run on with the ball, simply picked it up and handed it to the referee.

"Why did he do that?"

"Osgood was offside, the bloody fool."

"What's offside?"

"You see the Arsenal goalkeeper. Well, there has to be one other Arsenal player between him and a Chelsea player when— Oh, good shot."

"When what?"

"I can't explain now. Just watch, you'll pick it up."

She watched, but became more confused rather than picking it up. The whistle seemed to be blown so often, without her being able to understand the reason for it, and the occasional roars of approval and dismay didn't always seem to correspond with what was happening. A man beside her kept shouting, "Give it to Mary. Go on, Mary, get your powder puff out, why don't you bleedin' kiss 'im?" The man next to him said, "What a lot! They couldn't beat the blind school." She identified Mary as one of the Chelsea players, not conspicuous for his courage. The ball was bobbing about near the Arsenal goal, and she was going to ask James something about Mary, when a frightening roar filled the ground. Three or four Chelsea players embraced. Everybody around her was standing up and clapping. James was standing too, hands high above his head. She rose to her feet. She gathered that Chelsea had scored.

"What a goal!" said the man who had been talking about not being able to beat the blind school. "What a beautiful bloody bit of combination, eh?"

James leaned across her. "Hudson and Osgood playing the old one-two," he said.

The man on her other side nodded. "And Garland up for the finishing touch. Lovely. If they always played like that, eh?"

"If they did."

The game restarted. Sheila had noticed that one whole section of the crowd, a large red patch in the general blue sea, had neither stood nor clapped. Five minutes later Arsenal scored, to equalize. She was poised, ready to rise from her seat, but nobody stood up, and only those in the red patch showed excitement. The man next to her muttered, "What a defense! It's got that many holes it'd make a colander look watertight." Apart from this remark, she was surrounded by gloomy silence. She said to James, "They're very partisan, aren't they?"

"You should just go to Tottenham. Or up to Manchester. They think the only good opponent's a dead one. Here at Stamford Bridge they're mild, take it from me."

Her attention wandered. She looked at the people, and thought how extraordinary it was that grown men and women could get so excited about other people kicking a ball about. But perhaps it was she who was extraordinary. Perhaps it was a mark of the Natural Man to be absorbed in such things. What had Cro-Magnon Man felt about ball games? When had they first been played? Though it was not a matter of playing, she reflected, but of watching. Cro-Magnon Man might have played a ball game, but he would surely never have watched.

Her gaze roved the rows of faces below her, pale faces and dark ones, topped by flowing coils of hair or bald heads or caps and trilby hats. A man two rows ahead wore a trilby thick with grease and sweat. Were these watchers to be preferred to Cro-Magnon Man? Weren't they the junk of civilization?

In looking down and round, her attention had at one moment caught on something, as a lawnmower catches on a stone. She had flicked it aside and moved on. What was it? Something, somebody. She had seen somebody she recognized, or almost recognized. She began to look carefully down the rows of seats ahead and to the side. She realized what it was, saw it again, clutched James's arm. A whistle blew. One of the players picked up the ball, they trooped off the field. People around stood up, pushed toward the exit. The man next to her said, "Third Division stuff."

James agreed. "Good goal, though." He turned to her. "Half time. We can try to get a drink if you like, but there's a hell of a crowd—"

She was almost jumping up and down in excitement. "I've seen Rodríguez."

"Where?"

Her cheeks were flushed, her eyes sparkled, she looked positively pretty.

"A few rows down. Down there. But he's gone."

"You're sure it was Rodríguez?"

"Yes, he turned this way. And he was wearing that purple suit. You remember how mad he was about football. Perhaps he's in the bar."

"There's more than one, but they're all crowded." They went down the wooden steps, out of the stand, under the covered section, into a bar packed with people all talking at the tops of their voices. It was impossible even to see the counter, and Sheila flinched at the idea of trying to push a way through the crowd of mostly dirty and hostile-looking males.

"Why did you think I'd enjoy a place like this? It's like the Black Hole of Calcutta."

"You're always talking about Natural Man. Don't be so bloody prissy. And don't talk in clichés."

She turned her head away from him, saw Rodríguez walking past, and shrieked his name. They pushed toward the door, but conflicted with hopeful drink-seekers who were still pouring in. By the time they had got through, the man was a few yards away. He turned, and James recognized him.

Rodríguez began to run toward the exit, and they followed him, weaving a way through groups of boys standing about or walking aimlessly along. They were gaining, when a barrier of bodies formed before them. Sheila pushed a way forward, repeating "Excuse me." A blue arm held her back. A policeman said, "Not so fast, miss, *if* you please."

"But I must get through."

"In just a minute, miss."

Now there was a murmur from the crowd. She had never felt such frustration. "What is it?" she asked the man next to her.

"Dunno, love. Someone said it was the Dook of Edinburgh come to see some good soccer. 'E's come to the wrong shop."

Was it Prince Philip? She never knew, for the barrier of police constables suddenly disappeared, she was through and James with her, they were dodging among people toward the exit. But there was now no sign of the man they had been following. They stopped at the main gate, looked up and down the Fulham Road.

"Lost him."

"It *was* Rodríguez."

"Yes." He said with unaccustomed meekness, "You were clever to spot him."

"Just using my eyes. If saying that isn't a cliché."

"Not a cliché, a niggle. What do you suggest we do now?"

"Fulham Broadway tube station's down there to the right. If he doesn't live round here he might use that for a getaway. But I expect you want to go back to the match."

"I didn't know you had such a nice line in malice."

"Don't tell me you're prepared to give it up."

"I'm prepared to give it up."

They walked to the station, bought tickets and went onto the platform. They did not see Rodríguez. Later they went to the cinema and saw *The Last Picture Show*. She restrained herself from saying she loved it, because his verdict sounded so decisive. "Slick but sentimental." She was astonished by her own restraint, when she knew her opinion to be as good as or better than his, and decided that she really wanted him. But did he want her? It seemed very doubtful. At dinner she felt an unpleasant choking in her throat at sight of his profile when he turned to call the waiter, and reverted to her natural candor.

"Look, I've got this uncomfortable feeling when I see you doing things, and I know what it means is I fancy you. So if you don't like fat girls or you really are queer, you'd better say so."

He broke off a piece of bread stick. "You're not too fat."

"That's not what you said in Spain."

"You'd annoyed me."

"And anyway it isn't an answer."

"I just don't know about being queer. But we could try."

"Thanks again. Such enthusiasm."

"What do you want me to say? We can't go to bed here and

now, can we? Though if you're not hungry we could skip dinner. All right, I can see you don't want to, but don't tell me I'm cold-blooded. You're pretty cool yourself for a girl who's recently lost her father."

"I told you we didn't have an emotional relationship. And anyway, I'm not sure he's dead."

He took a mouthful of prawn cocktail, pointed the spoon at her. "But I have. Got an emotional relationship, I mean. Do you know who the prime suspect is going to be when they get down to it? My father. And it turns out that I have strong feelings about him. Does that surprise you?"

She did not care for people who pointed, especially with spoons, but when James did it her heart fluttered uneasily. "No, it doesn't."

"Why don't you go and see if that dental receptionist is the woman you saw in the teashop? And if she is, try and get something out of her?"

"All right."

"Only, of course, if a fiddle is being worked, your father must have had something to do with it. So perhaps I shouldn't ask."

"I'll talk to her. Next Monday."

"Terrific. And I'll tell Jerry about seeing Rodríguez. Though very likely they're onto him already."

"Will he be at home now? Your policeman friend?"

"It's Saturday. He won't be back till midnight, never is."

He paid the bill. As they went out of the restaurant he put an arm round her, then kissed her. "Now let's try to find the answer to that question, shall we?"

11

"You know the dictum of the excellent Sherlock Holmes. It should be in theory possible to sit back in the chair and solve any problem with what the good God has given to us here." Galera tapped his forehead.

"*This*, Gómez, is the finest computer in the world. Give it the full information and the correct conclusion will be reached. The question is, do we have the full information?"

Gómez was doing the filing. There was a great deal of it, almost all unimportant, referring to trivial thefts, long-drawn-out sagas of family assault and argument. In another organization it might have been done by a clerk, but everything that happened in the DIC was potentially of the highest importance. Gómez hesitated now before the responsibility of finding alphabetical order for St. Clair, Santa Clarabel, Sanivet and San Martín. Spelling was not his strong point, and how in any case should these Sans and Santas and Sts be placed? "They have not found this Rodríguez," he replied. "Here we should have found him."

The Jefe de Servicio lighted a black cheroot. He ignored Gómez's remark.

"Let us see what we know. First, the body is Rider, as proved by the teeth. Then, in these interviews conducted by our little Lieutenant Quevedo, it is obvious that Rider was at odds with his friend Paradine. And why? Our friends the English police tell us that Paradine has an affair with the woman, the wife. So it is a simple story, a crime of passion. Rider and Paradine quarrel, Paradine kills him, then he bribes Rodríguez to fix the body on the buoy. Then—listen to this carefully, Gómez, it is subtle—it occurs to Rodríguez that if the crime is known he can possibly blackmail Paradine. Do not tell me that this is conjecture, it is what makes sense. And what makes sense, Sherlock Holmes said, must be right although it appears improbable. If I could go to England myself, to question this Paradine and the woman—"

"But you cannot." Gómez spoke with satisfaction.

"The colonel lacks vision. My friends at Scotland Yard will ask more questions for me. But will they get the right answers?"

Gómez belched, loosened his belt. "I'll tell you what you want. You want Rodríguez."

Galera agreed. It went against nature for him to agree with Gómez, but he found himself reluctantly inclined to do so on this occasion.

12

At just about this time Alastair Stephenson drove up to Pevering Manor in his Jensen. As he entered the drive he passed a small dark man wearing an oddly colored suit who was leaving the house. Stephenson had never seen Rodríguez Orantes, and did not know that the police were looking for him. His business was with Amanda.

She received him in the green-and-gold drawing room. They drank China tea and ate cucumber sandwiches. She was as composed as usual. It would have been hard to say which of them was the calmer.

"Now that we know Roger is dead, a new situation is created. We ought to talk about it."

"I thought you'd come to express your sympathy."

Stephenson's hazel eyes looked into her green ones. "How much did you know about his business affairs? What did he tell you?"

"As much as a wife should know."

"Would it surprise you to know that he had siphoned an enormous amount of money out of the firm over the years? I don't know how much, but the amount's gigantic."

"It's easy to make accusations against a dead man." She bit into a sandwich. "And convenient."

"Shall I tell you how it was done?"

"I don't have the slightest interest. And I'm not prepared to listen to you blackening Roger's name."

Stephenson's mask of hauteur was touched by irritation. "For God's sake, Amanda, don't talk as if you were acting in one of those drawing-room comedies you always wanted to play in. This is serious, for you as well as me."

Now that he had spoken her name, she used his. "In that case, Alastair, hadn't you better tell me what you propose to do? I don't want any accusations or recriminations—keep them to yourself—but I am interested in any suggestions you want to make."

He wondered whether he should try to force her to listen to the whole story, or as much of it as he knew. Then he decided that perhaps she was right, and the less that was openly said, the better it would be for them both. So he kept to the things that had to be settled.

"Roger's holdings are around twenty percent. The Board's proposal is that we should buy them at half the current market figure. It's a unanimous proposal."

"They do what you tell them."

"I tell you, it's unanimous."

"*Half* the market figure. That seems a very poor price."

"I should say that in all the circumstances it's a handsome offer. If it had been left to me alone it would have been less."

She said demurely, "You forget that I don't know any of these circumstances."

He kept his temper with an effort. The increasing languor of her voice, almost a parody of his own, annoyed him. "Please. I said before that we aren't acting in a play."

"I don't know that I can accept this offer. I mean, why should I? I might like to retain my shares. I might even take an active interest in BMS."

"It will be difficult enough to keep BMS going. If you make it impossible you will suffer as much as anybody." His narrow head on its thin neck shot forward; he looked more than ever like a bird of prey. "One of the things agreed by the Board is that the whole Australian operation should be stopped for good. It's now closed down temporarily, but that will be permanent. I can tell you something else. Paradine has resigned, and his resignation will be accepted. Either he was ignorant of what happened, in which case he was a fool, or—"

"You need not go on," she said coolly. "I don't know what you're talking about."

"Amanda, in that case I'll tell you."

"Please. Nor do I *want* to know. We shall have to do it through solicitors, but you can take it that I accept the Board's offer."

The head drew back. "You're an intelligent woman."

In a voice so faint that it was almost inaudible she said, "Such praise. I'm truly complimented."

When he got up to go he said, "What will you do now? I can't imagine you staying here."

"Not my scene. I shall sell this house, probably the flat too. After that I haven't made up my mind, but I shan't stay in England. And I shan't worry you. We have an agreement."

The grip of her hand when they parted was cool but tight. In his imagination it was also rough, scaly, like that of a boa constrictor.

13

Sheila recognized Miss Shaw as soon as she came out of the dentist's chambers, followed her along crowded Oxford Street and was close behind when she entered a self-service café. So far, so easy. Miss Shaw picked up a tray and moved along the queue with practiced skill, taking roll, butter, steak pie and vegetables, like a bird in the nest gulping down gifts with open beak. Sheila, unused to the system, was past the rolls and butter before she realized it, hesitated in front of the hot dishes and moved on without taking any of them because of the powerful pressure from would-be eaters behind her, and at last snatched a dismal-looking plate of salad. Had she lost the quarry? A look round showed Miss Shaw sitting at a table on her own. Sheila made her way to it, brushed away an accumulation of crumbs with one hand, and looked round in bewilderment. Nobody except herself appeared to have a tray.

"Could you tell me—"

Miss Shaw looked up from her *Daily Mirror* and made a gesture toward a pile of trays. Sheila put hers with the rest, and contemplated her cottage cheese, grated carrot and lettuce with distaste. She realized she had forgotten to take a knife and fork.

"Would you mind—my knife and fork—looking after—"

Miss Shaw looked up again. "Okay."

In getting the knife and fork Sheila felt like a salmon swimming against the current, but at last she managed it. Miss Shaw acknowledged her return with a nod. The lettuce had the consistency of rubber, the carrot tasted vaguely of some chemical. Well, she thought, it's better for me than a lot of starch. On Saturday night James had made an ungallant remark about her figure, although the evening had been in other ways highly satisfactory. Brooding on this, she forgot why she was in the café until she noticed with alarm that Miss Shaw had finished her steak pie and was drinking coffee.

How to start? "It's the first time I've come here." No reply. "These places are very mechanical, aren't they? We're like a lot of battery hens."

"It's quick," Miss Shaw said. Her coffee cup was three-quarters empty.

Sheila spoke desperately. "Miss Shaw."

The other girl looked up. Her face was the color of white paper slightly soiled. Even the thin lips lacked color.

Sheila went on. "Miss Shaw, I'm Sheila Rider. You knew my father."

The girl drained her coffee, folded her paper, pushed her chair back.

"I saw you with him once. Coming out of a café like this one. I spoke to him and you were with him."

"Must have been somebody else."

When she spoke these words and got up, Sheila knew positively that the other woman had something to hide. Her natural resolution returned. "You'd better sit down. You wouldn't want me to talk to the police." Miss Shaw sat down, still gripping her newspaper tightly. "That dental chart you gave to the police. My father made some arrangement with you about it, didn't he? The chart belonged to somebody else."

"I'm not going to talk about it."

"Don't be stupid." Sheila felt suddenly fully in command of the situation, and the sensation was enjoyable. "If I tell the police you've been meeting my father you'll be in all sorts of trouble. I want to find out if he's dead or alive."

Small washed-out blue eyes in the pale face looked at her cautiously. Miss Shaw looked like a white rat in a corner. "He could be alive. If it's just the dental identification."

"You mean the chart did belong to somebody else."

The white rat suddenly leaped from its corner. "It's all right for you, you never had to worry about money. I've got two kids, both under five, and the bastard I was living with just cleared out, left me with them. They're at nursery school so that I can go out to a job. Do you know how much that costs?"

"I'm not interested in—"

"You know nothing, bloody nothing! People like you make me sick. Do you think I can afford to waste food like that?" She pointed to Sheila's almost untouched salad, opened a bag, took out a packet of cigarettes.

"I'm glad you can manage to buy cigarettes." The white rat glared at her. "I don't care what you've done. I'm just trying to find out what happened to my father. He asked you to destroy his dental chart and put in another one, is that it? Did he say why?"

"Why should I care? He paid for it, that's all I know."

"How much? Though it doesn't matter."

The white rat blew a cigarette ring. "I don't mind you knowing. He paid two fifty. In notes." She added with pride, "I wouldn't take a check."

"So you just destroyed his chart and put in this other one."

"It was more than that. It wouldn't have worked at all, except that old Mr. Smith had retired. I had to destroy the record card, because it wouldn't have been the same as the new chart. And then I had to type up the new chart. It wasn't money for nothing."

"The chart you copied from. There must have been a name on it. Do you remember that?"

The little eyes looked sideways at Sheila. For a moment she thought that Miss Shaw was going to ask for money. Then she said, "I'll tell you one funny thing. The chart, the one I copied, was Australian. They're not quite the same as ours, so I noticed. The name, though, I don't remember that. It began with S, and it was something to do with the sun. Sunley, Sunder, Sunnick—"

"Summers?"

"Right, Summers. Satisfied?" She stubbed out her cigarette.

"I'll tell you something. You ought to go to the police with this. If they find it out themselves you'll really be in trouble."

She left Miss Shaw sitting at the table. As soon as she got home she telephoned James.

14

"Do you mean you think Roger wanted to have me suspected of killing him?" Geoffrey stared at his son.

"I think he planned the whole thing. He invented a plan to kill Roger Rider, with you as chief suspect. It was really a plot against you."

"I can't believe he would have done that."

"Just think, dad. He knew about your affair with his wife, though he never mentioned it to you. He asked you out to Spain, which he'd never done before. He wanted to disappear because he was in financial trouble, but if he just vanished the police would be after him. So he had to die, and because of your affair with Amanda he picked you as his murderer. Perhaps because of other things too. There must have been a lot of hatred in that old-friends routine."

"Perhaps there was. Perhaps I was getting back at him myself through the affair with Amanda." His glance strayed to the chessboard on its table beside his armchair. "Do you know, I believe I've found an absolute answer to one of Fischer's attacking ploys? It's one he used against Larsen, and again against Petrosian—"

"Don't tell me you aren't interested. If Sheila hadn't found this dental receptionist, showing that Rider planned to disappear, you'd have been in all sorts of trouble."

"Don't think I'm ungrateful to you," his father said apologetically. "Or to her. It's just—well, you know I've resigned from BMS, and all that kind of thing seems totally in the past, somehow unreal." He brightened momentarily. "I've started to write again. My memoirs. I'm calling them *The Story of a Non-Existent Man*. Don't you think that's rather good?"

"Dad. There are some questions I want to ask, about BMS. Do you think you can just concentrate on *that* for ten minutes?"

"I suppose so," his father said reluctantly.

"You were the head of Foreign Sales."

"I was called that. For what it was worth."

"But Rider handled part of it himself, the drug sales to Australia, right?"

"To the whole subcontinent through our Australian agents, yes. It's really most extraordinary that Hubert should have been mixed up in all that."

"I believe Rider did that deliberately, so that if there was any trouble you'd be implicated. Dad, are you going to listen to me?"

"I'm listening."

"My idea comes from the thesis I'm doing on real-life and fictional crime. I've been reading about American frauds, and one of them was done by a man named Philip Musica. He was a swindler who changed his name, started a drug firm and then bought up lots of others. They seemed to be making huge profits, the price of the stock went up, they kept on expanding. Are you following me?"

His father was flaking a piece of dry skin off the back of his left hand with the nail of his right index finger. "Expanded, yes."

"The whole thing was a fraud. It was done like this. Musica handled the crude-drug department. They bought drugs in Canada which were invoiced to them through Manning's Bank in Montreal, and then sold them through a company in Montreal which had offices all over the world. The profits on paper were gigantic. But in fact they didn't exist. None of it existed except on paper. Manning's Bank was a small office with one woman in it; the selling company was another room just down the road with one typist. The object of the operation was to increase the value of the shares. Musica was paying blackmail to a lot of people, and in the end things got too difficult and he committed suicide." He took a deep breath. "I think Rider was carrying on a Musica type of operation."

Geoffrey Paradine had removed the piece of skin. Now he flicked it away. "But he didn't kill himself. You say he's alive."

Was his father being deliberately obtuse? "Perhaps I'm explaining it badly. The important question is this: if Rider had wanted to work this kind of fraud through Intertrade and Austro-Asian Products, could he have done it? There would have been a big paper profit, and BMS would apparently have accumulated materials worth a lot of money, but in fact the materials wouldn't exist. Roger would just have been bleeding the firm. Now, could he have done it?"

"I suppose so. I really don't know."

"A woman named Swan was killed by a hit-and-run driver. She worked for Austro-Asian. Have you ever heard of her?"

"I'm afraid I haven't."

"I found part of a letter in Uncle Hubert's writing which suggests that she was killed, and that Summers was employed to do it."

His father shook his head like a man coming up out of water.

148

"If Roger's alive, where do you think he is now?"

"He might be anywhere, in a French village or on Copacabana beach, but I believe he's in England. Rodríguez came over here, and he must have hoped to get in touch with Roger. But, dad, *could* it all have happened the way I'm saying? Could Roger have used you like that?"

Geoffrey Paradine sighed. "I'm afraid he could. The truth is, my boy, that I wasn't cut out to be a businessman."

15

One of Jerry's more infuriating habits was to cook himself a meal and then clear away only part of it, so that a dirty teacup or a plate marked with congealed bacon fat would be left on the table. When James returned from Kentish Town a small jug of cream, a bowl of sugar and a dish containing banana peel were the first things he saw. Propped up against the sugar bowl was a letter from the Banco Grande de la República Argentina in Buenos Aires. It began "Dear Mr. Maitland," said that the position of Head of the Security Department, with over-all responsibility for all social affairs, had again become vacant at the salary previously offered, and that the undersigned personally hoped very much that he would consider it. The undersigned proved to be J. Hernández Rawson, the managing director. At the top of the letter Jerry had scrawled "How about that?" Beside the words "Salary previously offered" he had written "£6000 plus and car," and at the bottom "What do you advise? Back about 10:30."

James cleared away the things, and went across to take a piece of paper from the pad beside the telephone so that he could write a reply. The top sheet had half a dozen notes written on it. Two were girls' names with telephone numbers, another gave train times for Bristol, another still said: "Rodríguez, 57d Peterbridge

Square." James looked for the London gazetteer which should have been on a shelf containing reference books, found it on Jerry's bedside table beneath a copy of *The Three Musketeers* and discovered that Peterbridge Square was between Islington and Stoke Newington. A bus map showed that a 30 bus would take him near it. He wrote a note:

Have *cleared up* after you. J. Hernández wouldn't offer that much if he knew your filthy domestic habits. Advise making sure he really exists, and isn't mental-home patient. Going on scouting expedition, see you on return. J.

Half an hour later the bus decanted him in an area of large shabby-faced houses that regretted the dignity of their Victorian past. In Peterbridge Square itself there were a few dusty plane trees and a children's playground in the center made from what had once been a garden. Colored boys leaned against lamp posts talking and giggling in low voices. At one place half a dozen of them blocked the pavement. It would have been possible to pass them by going into the road, but why should he do that? At the last moment they parted to let him through. A low whistle followed him.

A light above a fanlight said 57. He went up a dozen worn gray steps to the front door, and found it shut. There was not much light, but he was able to see at one side a row of bells with letters beside them from A to F. He pressed the bell marked D. For a few seconds there was no reply. Then a buzzer sounded. He pushed the door and it opened. He stepped inside.

The hall smelled of something, not exactly of drains or food, but a blend of spices and stale water. The smell clung like a texture to the acid-green distemper on the walls, it had penetrated the grayish white of the ceiling. He put his feet on the uncarpeted stairs and had gone up half the first flight when the light went out.

Darkness. In the darkness the smell. And in the darkness it seemed that somebody was breathing. He knew that the light would be controlled by a time switch and that he had simply failed to press this switch, but suddenly he was afraid. It was a sensation that he could not remember feeling before, and it was not entirely disagreeable, a heightening of feeling so that when he put out fingers to touch the wall it seemed to have some living responsive texture. In his stomach something appeared to have curled up, a small animal. *A kitten curled up in my stomach and purring*, he thought.

He felt his way up to a landing, and met roundness with a nipple at its center. He pressed the nipple. Light came on, subdued, but enough to make visible doors saying A and B. In the blankness of the doors little spyholes stared at him. He could hear the time switch ticking.

The kitten remained in his stomach as he went up the next flight of stairs. The smell remained, covering everything like smog. The doors stood facing each other, saying C and D. Again they contained spyholes, and at the side of each door was a bell. He was about to press the bell of D when it occurred to him that he did not know what to say to Rodríguez. An open accusation that he had helped to dispose of Summers, a suggestion that the man could talk either to him or to Scotland Yard, perhaps an offer of help if the Spaniard told him where to get hold of Rider? The flat was dark. Since Rodríguez knew that somebody was coming up, would it not have been natural to turn on the light inside and open the door?

He pressed the bell. And, as it seemed at the very moment of pressure, the light went out again.

He felt that somebody else was with him on the stairs, that if he reached out to push the nipple, another hand would silently close over his. The door of D was faintly visible in front of him. Since Rodríguez had let him into the house, why did he not let him into the flat?

He was no longer faced by total blackness. What had happened? He felt for the door, and it was not there. A voice whispered "Rodríguez," and a moment passed before he identified it as his own.

Then he stepped forward boldly into blackness, felt for a light switch and found it. Dingy yellow light illuminated a purple-suited figure on the floor. Then a clap of thunder sounded inside his head, and everything had gone.

In a room. On a bed, not *in* a bed. Clothes? Yes, wearing clothes. Then why on a bed? A voice said, "Hi." He opened his eyes. Jerry grinned down at him.

He let eyes wander about the room. Bare walls, people passing, a hospital. "Why not in bed?"

"What? Oh, yes, I see. Because you've got a thick skull. You were hit on the head, and they brought you here in case you were concussed, but you don't look any more idiotic than usual to me. Which is not saying much. Try sitting up."

He tried. His head hurt, but he did not feel dizzy. "I'm all right. What happened? I went to see Rodríguez."

"You got the address off the pad in the flat, I suppose? I thought so. You know what will happen if you keep sticking that handsome nose into what's none of your business, don't you? It'll get cut off. When did you get there?"

"Just after nine."

"I was there at ten fifteen. Had to see a man about some con trick a firm of car dealers is working out at Edgware. Found you on the floor inside the room. Somebody beat us both to it."

"Rodríguez is—"

"Rodríguez is dead. Shot once through the head. No sign of a weapon. Chummy probably used it to hit you on the head, then walked out. Now, I'm not here just to take you home, though I'll do that. The important thing is this. Did you get a look at him?" James shook his head, which proved painful. "A glimpse, a smell, did he say anything, did you see anything, anything at all?"

"Nothing. He must have stood behind the door. It was dark on the landing, and I got a bit nervous. Like a fool, I walked in, switched on the light and got cracked on the head. I just caught sight of Rodríguez on the floor, that's all."

"Like a fool. A very well-chosen phrase. All right, cocker, let's go home."

In the car James started to tell Jerry his theory about Rider and Philip Musica, but found his head aching and his speech becoming incoherent. When Jerry said it would keep, he was thankful to stop, more thankful still to undress, take two pain-killers and get into bed. Jerry looked at him with concern, went away, returned with a cup of tea. James sipped the strong sweet mixture gratefully. Jerry sat on the bed and James was interested that he felt no stir of sexual feeling. Was he too feeble, or had Sheila effected a cure?

"I've got to go out again, see what the boys have turned up. Sure you're okay?"

"Fine. One thing, Jerry. Rodríguez's address, where did it come from?"

"Anonymous phone call here. Man's voice. Just gave the address and rang off. I'll tell you something else. The Sydney police have talked to the woman Summers lived with, and she knew the name of his dentist. Four months ago he had a break-in, lost a few of his instruments, nothing else taken, couldn't understand it. What's the betting the object of the exercise was to take a Xerox copy of Summers' dental chart?"

"Interesting." He closed his eyes, opened them again. "What about that job?"

Jerry was at the door. He turned, smiling. "Wondered when you'd remember that. Still haven't made up my mind."

16

In the morning James had a lump on the back of his head, but otherwise felt perfectly well. Jerry filled him in on the case at breakfast.

"Rodríguez seems to have holed up in that room since he came over. Nobody there knew anything about him, or whether he had visitors. Nothing in his wallet that gives any clue to what he came over for. His forged passport was the kind you can get in any big city if you have the cash and know where to go. Altogether, you might call him a dead end."

"I think I know what he'd come for." He gave Jerry an account of Sheila's interview with the dental receptionist, and his own ideas about Rider creating a plot against himself, ending with his murder. Jerry listened with a look on his face that became increasingly gloomy.

"That's it then, isn't it?" he said when James had finished.

"How d'you mean?"

"All that stuff about Miss Shaw. I should have got onto it. Anyone bright would have done. Maitland didn't. Conclusion, Maitland's not very bright." He had got out his pencil, and was digging away at the plastic table mat on which the coffee jug stood.

"That's ridiculous. It just happens Sheila had seen her father with this girl in a café, that's all. That reminds me, I must ring Sheila up."

"She rang you, early this morning. I told her what happened to you. Sounded concerned. Sort of girl you ought to marry to keep you out of mischief."

"It's not easy to dig a hole in plastic, but you might manage it if you go on." Jerry stopped digging. The pencil snapped between his fingers. "You really mean it, don't you?"

"What?"

"About that girl Miss Shaw. But you're wrong. Our finding out was a pure piece of luck."

"Then put me down as unlucky. That means I'm no good." Jerry put his arms on the table, looked across it intently. "When you're a detective you're supposed to have a special sort of skill. You may not be a great brain, but you know when people are telling the truth, or at least when they're telling obvious lies. I ought to have smelled something wrong when she said the notes had been destroyed. But I didn't, don't you see, I didn't. I was just bloody stupid." He thumped one hand into the palm of the other. "So that's it."

"How do you mean?"

"I'm taking the job in B.A. Let's face it, what future is there for a sergeant who lets himself be outsmarted by some nut writing a thesis about crime?"

They argued for another ten minutes before Jerry left for Scotland Yard. After he had gone, James noticed that all the breakfast things had been left for him to clear away.

Jerry used the same argument when putting the letter from J. Hernández Rawson in front of Feathers, along with his resignation. He had already told the superintendent about his error in relation to Miss Shaw, and about James's theories.

Feathers listened impassively, then sat back. "You don't want to decide a thing like this in a hurry, boy."

"This won't wait." Jerry tapped the letter.

"If they want you they'll wait."

"Six thousand plus—when am I going to make that kind of money? Two years I'll get made up to Inspector, if I'm lucky. Five years after that I could make Super, if all the cards fall right. Seven, eight or ten would be more likely. That's the end of it, and would I be making six thousand plus then? You bloody know I wouldn't."

"If all you want is money, there's easier ways of making it." Feathers folded the letter, handed it back. "But if you're a jack, that's what you are, and it's what you want to be. Head of Security, responsibility for social affairs, what's it mean but you're going to be eyes and ears for a lot of wogs? Is that what you want? I never thought so or you'd not have been on my team, you know that." Maitland moved restlessly. "Just hear me out, boy. Now, these fancy ideas your chum's got—may be something in them, may not. This Spaniard getting it changes the whole case, it gives us an interest, we'll really start looking for Rider. But, like he says, I don't see any way you were to know about the girl. If you'd spotted it, all right. But missing it, I don't hold that against you."

"If I hadn't gone to see that little shit Gunter last night, if I'd gone straight to Peterbridge Square—"

"And if I grew tits and looked different I might be a film star. I don't hold that against you either. You're a good jack, Jerry." Feathers turned away, blew his nose hard. "If you take this job with the wogs they'll be lucky. I'm telling you I'll be sorry."

"Just the same." Jerry dug with his pencil into the pad in front of him. "You've got my letter of resignation."

"You mean you want me to act on it?" Feathers glared at him. His red face was angry, his eyes dry. He got up, went to the window, stood with his back to Maitland. "I don't blame you. They want a good police force, they talk about getting the right sort into it, then when they've got 'em, what do they use for money? Peanuts. For me it's not the same, I was brought up with it and haven't got long to go, but why should you stay? If you get shot the bastard who did it is sent to a head-shrinker to see if his mother used to play with his trigger finger when he was a baby. Do something a bit swift and you're on the carpet. Make a deal with a couple of little fish to catch the big one and some smart-arse lawyer says you've fixed him. What's in it for you? What's in it for any copper but grief?" He came back to his desk, read the resignation letter again, tore it in half and dropped it in a wastepaper basket. "Just the same, I'd like you to hold it over for a couple of days. Your chum in the Argentine will wait that long."

"It'll be the same then as it is now."

"Maybe. But the Spaniard getting himself wiped out changes things, you see that. We've got a crime on our own ground, and we can do something about it. You've questioned your friend Paradine about whether he saw anything?"

"Yes. Nothing at all. He just walked in the room and was hit from behind."

"He was shot with an automatic, just one shot through the head, neat enough. Lots of marks about, but we don't know if any of them are linked with the killing because we don't have any dabs of the people except Rider and your friend's father, and they don't fit. This idea that Rider milked the firm for years, what do you think of it?"

"It fits in with the tale I was told. And it could be why Stephenson choked me off."

"I think it's time we had another chat with Mr. Stephenson. Together. And it might be an idea to talk to Mrs. Rider again." His imagination lingered over this second prospect.

17

When Feathers wished, he could adopt a manner halfway between prosecution counsel and hanging judge. He used this manner now in talking to Stephenson.

"Sergeant Maitland asked you earlier whether Rider had any financial problems, and whether there was any trouble inside the firm. You said you knew of nothing. Do you want to adhere to that answer, Mr. Stephenson?"

Stephenson touched the knot of his tie, but showed no other mark of nervousness. "Yes."

"My information is that there was something very wrong with your operations in Australia. Do you wish to comment on that?"

The hawklike head turned from one to the other of them. "The man's dead. What's the purpose of dragging up something that can be nothing but damaging to the firm?"

"I'm trying to be considerate, sir. If you'd prefer to answer questions at Scotland Yard, all right." Stephenson did not reply. Feathers stood up. "Get your coat."

"Sit down, superintendent."

"Are *you* telling *me* to do something?"

"I'm sorry. All I've been trying to do is to protect the company. Rider's been robbing it, had been for years. He had a whole phony set-up out in Sydney, two imaginary subsidiaries that bought and sold imaginary goods and made imaginary profits."

Feathers and Maitland exchanged glances. The sergeant said, "Intertrade and Austro-Asian Products?"

"You know about them? Then why ask me?"

Feathers broke in. "How do *you* know? That's the important thing. And *when* did you know? And what did you do about it?"

"A man who called himself Princeton rang me up one day—"

"When?"

"Shortly before Rider left for Spain. He said he had something important to tell me personally. He was supposed to be in charge of the Intertrade office."

"And he was Geoffrey Paradine's brother Hubert. We know all about him. What did he suggest?"

"He told me what had been going on. At first I didn't believe it, but he went into such a hell of a lot of detail that I was convinced. He threatened to make the whole thing public, and wanted ten thousand pounds to keep quiet. I told him he could whistle. If you once start paying blackmail it never ends."

"And had he talked to Rider?"

"Rider told him that if he brought BMS down he'd be in jail himself for a long term, which was true enough. He refused to pay anything."

"So then you talked to Rider?"

"Yes."

"And what did he say?"

"At first he tried to bluff it out, said there was nothing in what Princeton had been telling me. When I said we must have a full investigation of the accounts, he changed his tune. He'd been doing it for years, long before I joined BMS. I know what you're going to ask: how did he get away with it in the accounts? Well, you can get away with almost anything nowadays in the way of paper profits if you talk fast enough and use the right accountant." A smile glinted briefly and was gone. "I should know, I'm one myself."

"But when you came into the firm, you didn't check up?"

Stephenson smiled again. "You must know, superintendent, that a check of that sort takes months. I trusted Rider. There's no reason why I shouldn't have done."

"Wasn't there ever any trouble?"

"Earlier this year I suggested that we should reduce the amount of stock Intertrade had accumulated. The figure shown in the accounts seemed to me far too big. A couple of months later Rider told me this had been done. Since no stock existed, he'd just made a paper sale through Austro-Asian. Of course the problem would have come up again next year. He'd just postponed it."

"That girl in Paradine's office must have been bright to spot something wrong," Feathers said to Maitland. Stephenson looked inquiring. The sergeant did not reply. Instead he asked, "How much was Geoffrey Paradine mixed up in it?"

The hawk's head bobbed up and down. "A good question. He was in charge of the department. Rider wouldn't say how much he knew, but conveyed without saying so that he was in it up to the neck. I don't believe that was true, I think Rider just used him. He's resigned, I told you that."

Feathers asked, "What happened after your showdown with Rider?"

"I told him that I wanted him out. That was the first thing. I insisted on it."

"What was his reaction?"

"He agreed to resign as soon as he came back from Spain, said he wanted a little while to put things in order. A few weeks more or less made no difference. I told him there'd be a full-scale investigation once he was gone, and that he'd have to pay back at least some of the money. He knew we wouldn't want to see him in the dock."

"You just thought about the firm?"

Stephenson did not seem to detect any irony. "That's right."

"And have you started the inquiry?"

"You understand there can't be any scandal, otherwise the shares would start slipping, and a slip like that can become an avalanche. There's nothing basically wrong with BMS. The trading figures next year are going to look pretty sick, but with luck we shall get away with them. If there's no scandal, that is."

Feathers looked at Stephenson and then spoke, with anger throbbing in his voice like the wind through telephone wires. "When Sergeant Maitland came to see you, you knew all this."

"He asked me whether Rider had any financial problems. I said he hadn't. He must have a lot of money stowed away. And he asked whether there was trouble inside the firm. There wasn't. There isn't. And if it rests with me there won't be."

"What you've done is called obstructing police inquiries."

"I call it protecting the interests of my shareholders. You aren't one of them, I suppose? If you were, you'd appreciate my action. Or perhaps if you'd come yourself in the first place? I don't like talking to underlings."

"Don't push me too far. There's nothing I'd like more than to take you in." Feathers was on his feet again. He walked across the room, an aging man but still formidable, and stood glaring at Stephenson. "If I find one thing, just one little thing, that you've been holding out on me, I'll smack you down so hard you won't know whether you're here or in the middle of next week."

Stephenson managed his smile, but only just. "If the Duke of Wellington were here, he'd say I don't know what the police do to criminals, but by God they terrify me. But I see the reference escapes you. Perhaps there's one other thing I ought to tell you. I've arranged with the sorrowing widow to buy her husband's shares at half the market price. I think a fair deduction would be that she knew just what he was doing, don't you?"

Feathers made a sign to Maitland, who got to his feet. At the door the superintendent paused. "I shouldn't be in too much of a hurry to make that deal. It might not be valid. Or the shares may be worth nothing. It's quite likely that Rider's still alive."

He had the pleasure of leaving while Stephenson's mouth was still slightly open.

18

"It's a ball of malt you take, isn't it?" Amanda's black dress was cut so that it just failed to reveal her breasts. Feathers' gaze was drawn as by a magnet to this curving area of flesh. She turned to Maitland, eyebrows lifted.

"If you've got a beer."

"Of course. Whisky for the super, beer for the sergeant, very proper." She gave him beer, poured tonic water for herself.

"It's not automatic," Feathers said. "You've got a good memory, Mrs. Rider. About the whisky, I mean."

"Thank you."

"I should have thought you'd have remembered to tell me your husband was planning to disappear."

"I don't understand."

Maitland spoke savagely. "Don't let a frown wrinkle that pretty forehead. You knew exactly what he was doing, didn't you? About his milking the company, and the fact that he'd been found out."

"All right, Jerry." Feathers did not approve of the harsh tone, nor of the amount the sergeant had given away. "Let's take it step by step, shall we? Did you know your husband was in deep trouble at BMS, and that he'd agreed to resign?"

"Because the way he'd been milking the firm through the Australian end had been found out," said the irrepressible Maitland.

"I thought something was wrong. I didn't know any details," she said with unbroken calmness. "I said to Alastair Stephenson that Roger had told me just as much as he wanted me to know. I knew he was worried, that's all. Then one day last week Alastair came down to see me at Pevering Manor. He wanted to buy Roger's holding at half the market price. I agreed."

If you put a hand inside that dress, Feathers thought, they

would pop out like ripe peaches. It was with less emphasis than he intended that he said, "You agreed?"

She moved a little in the bubble chair. "I never like to haggle, I'm not a bargainer. Alastair told me something was wrong. I didn't want to know the details, I wanted to get rid of the shares. So I agreed. Does it seem so surprising?"

With an effort Feathers removed his mind from thought of the nipple that stood out under the black dress. He remembered her tactic of answering one question with another, and ignored this one. "I'll go back to what I said first of all. There's a lot of evidence suggesting that your husband proposed to solve his troubles by disappearing while he was in Spain. Do you know whether he had such an intention? Think carefully before you answer."

Maitland had his notebook out. She looked bewildered. "I don't understand. Surely Roger's dead? I understood he'd been —killed."

"It is possible he may be alive." Feathers was watching her closely. Her look of pleasure and surprise seemed perfectly genuine.

"That's wonderful. Can I talk to him? I'd better take off these widow's weeds first, though, hadn't I?" She gave a brief giggle.

Feathers had the feeling that the interview was slipping away from him. "I said it was a possibility, that's all. And I'm still waiting for an answer. Did you know he planned to disappear?"

"No."

"He hasn't been in touch with you?"

"Obviously not. Do you mean somebody's seen him?"

He ignored this question too. "Mrs. Rider, I put it to you that you knew about his plan to make it look as though he had been murdered, and to suggest that Geoffrey Paradine had a strong motive for killing him." In his best heavyweight voice he went on, "At present I don't know of anything to suggest that you helped him. If he's alive he'll have to talk to us. If you have any idea where he might be you'll help him and yourself by telling us now."

She leaned forward in the bubble chair. The peaches seemed to be glued within the black dress. "This is all because that little man Rodríguez has been killed, isn't it?"

"Don't ask me things," he said harshly. "Just answer the questions. Have you heard from him?"

"I have not. And, superintendent, I should be glad if you'd let me know when you've made up your mind whether Roger is still alive and you suspect him of being mixed up in a murder, or dead and murdered by somebody else. At present, you seem to me confused."

With that Feathers had to rest content. Or, rather, he rested very discontented, for they got no more out of her. He felt that he should have handled the interview more incisively, and certainly Jerry's interventions had been no help.

"I was trying to tease her along. When you said Rider had been milking the company, we lost any chance of surprise."

"Shock tactics. I know they didn't work."

"When I'm running an interview, Jerry, *I* decide the tactics."

"Sorry. I seem to make a balls of everything lately. You'll be glad to get shot of me."

Feathers ignored this. "Just let's see the way it could have happened. We still don't know for certain that it did. Rider had it all planned for a long time, back to the point when he arranged to get hold of Summers' dental chart. He gets Summers over to Spain on the pretext that he's got a job for him. From the way Summers talked to Mrs. Rider, he'd probably been told that the job was to knock her off. In fact Rider's setting Summers up as victim, to be identified as Rider through the dental details. Agreed so far?" Jerry nodded. "At the same time he wants a mug to act as suspect, and what better patsy is there than his old friend Geoff, who's already served as cover for his Australian operation? All the more reason, too, when he learns that Amanda's having it away with Geoff. Though me, I'd say you'd be safer having it away with a black mamba."

"All according to taste."

"Yeah, plenty of black mambas in the Argentine, they tell me. Still making sense?"

"Still making sense."

"The spanner in the works is Hubert, who guesses what's going on—very likely he's arranged for Summers to come over —and turns up asking for his cut. Rider brushes him off, something he can afford to do because in a few days he'll have disappeared. But then Hubert comes to Spain, makes veiled threats and has to be dealt with. So Rider dopes him or has it done by Rodríguez, dopes some of the other people at the house party. He gets rid of Hubert with the help of Rodríguez and Summers. But Summers is for the chop too, and gets it probably when they return to the village. They take him out to sea, fix him to the buoy. Mission accomplished. Then Rodríguez tries to put the black on Rider and he's disposed of too. How does it sound?"

"Fine. Except that you can't prove any of it."

"The proof, my boy, comes when we catch friend Roger. And how do we do that? Put an alert out for him, and, above all, keep a tail on the black mamba, put a tap on her phone. I'd like you to handle this yourself. When she makes a move to leave the country, bring her in for questioning."

Maitland stared. "Why not tell her she isn't free to leave? Call in her passport."

Feathers tapped his nose. "Give her rope, she'll be all the more likely to lead us to Rider. Has it occurred to you that she may be in this up to the neck? That she went to bed with Paradine just to incriminate him as a suspect later on, and that Rider knew about it from the start?"

"Do you believe that?"

"I'm not sure. But I'll tell you something. There's better ways of catching a black mamba than trying to frighten it to death."

On this occasion, however, they did not catch the black mamba. Jerry was one of the four tails who worked on the assignment, and it was Jerry who lost her. Or, rather, she lost him. She did it quite easily in Harrod's by going up on the escalator and then immediately down in a lift. No doubt she'd seen him following her, but was she determined to shake him or had she arranged to meet somebody? Jerry asked Feathers. For another few hours, they believed that she was still in England, until a pilot running his own little private airline said that he had taken her to an airfield near Paris. She had made her booking with him in advance, and was out of the country within an hour of giving Jerry the slip.

That was not the last Feathers heard of her. Five days after her departure he received a postcard giving a hotel address in Paris, which said, "Kept seeing that Sergeant of yours, isn't London a small place. Perhaps Paris is bigger. Staying Hotel Suisse if you need me." The Paris police found that she had left the hotel on the morning she sent the card. Another card came from Florence, again naming a hotel, and again she had left before the card got to Scotland Yard. She was plainly an elusive black mamba.

Anybody might have lost her, but it had been Jerry Maitland who did, and, as he said to Feathers, that was the last straw. He told the superintendent that he was taking the job in Buenos Aires, and the second resignation he wrote out was accepted.

When Jerry told him the news, James at first did not believe it.

"You must be out of your mind."

"I'm celebrating." He gestured toward whisky on the table. "Pour your own. Or there's beer in the fridge." Jerry had a wild look in his eye. He did not look as if he was enjoying his own celebration.

"All right then, good luck. If it's what you want."

"Which of us doesn't want money?"

"I'll miss you, Jerry." Looking at the bullet head and sturdy body, he felt a twinge of the physical affection he thought he had outgrown.

"Shall I tell you something? The person I shall miss most in this bastard country is you. We've had some good times, haven't we?"

James sat down with his whisky. "You're sure about it?"

"I'm not sure of anything, except that I've got no future as a copper. So—" He waved a hand, and James realized that he was slightly drunk. "So I've seen J. Hernández or his representative, and said yes. Buenos Aires, here I come. Next Tuesday."

This was on a Friday. "As soon as that?"

"The Metropolitan Police Force having been graciously pleased to accept my resignation, what's to keep me? I'll tell you something, boy. Old Gilbert and Sullivan were right, a policeman's lot is not a happy one. I'm sorry."

"What for?"

"Everything. Well, I mean about the flat and all that, leaving you on your own. If I give you a month's rent, will that be all right?"

"Of course. As a matter of fact, Sheila and I have been talking about sharing a flat. I was going to say something to you, because this one's a bit small. But now that you're going—"

"Congratulations, my old James. Never met her, but I know she's a nice girl. I'll drink to her." They drank to Sheila. "Don't worry about my gear, I'll have everything packed up and out of the way by the weekend."

After this they settled down to serious drinking. It was midnight when they staggered off to bed.

On Tuesday James went to Heathrow and saw Jerry off. He met there a brick-faced burly man introduced as "Feathers, who used to be my boss." After they had said their goodbyes and walked away, the superintendent spoke.

"Bloody fool, that boy. He had a great future. But there you are, he wanted everything too fast. You're all the same, all of you." As they came out into the entrance hall he said, "You're the lad who found out about the dental chart."

"Not me, really, it was Rider's daughter. She happened to remember—"

"I heard it from Jerry. And it was your bright idea that Rider fixed everything to show that he'd been killed, and to incriminate your father." James said modestly that it was. "Jerry fell for that, hook, line and sinker. One of the things that upset him was he felt he ought to have thought of it first. It all seemed to hang together nicely, I'll grant you that. Only thing is, on the latest information we've got, it seems to have been wrong."

"Wrong?" James said unbelievingly. "I don't understand."

Over a beer in the airport bar, Feathers told him.

19

The report that Orantes had been killed in London left Manuel Galera deeply depressed. He had built up in his mind a precise picture of the course which events would take. The arrest of Orantes by the efficient London police, his return to Spain, the interrogation which would reveal that he had been paid by Geoffrey Paradine to act as accessory to the murder, the request for Paradine's extradition, and, as a triumphant finale to the affair, his own visit to England to collect the prisoner, congratulations from the Scotland Yard officer on his deductive genius, long sessions in the London pubs that he liked so much in which the Scotland Yard detectives listened respectfully to his analysis of the case, a final interview with the commissioner himself.

He had to acknowledge now that this bubble picture was a long, long way from reality. Scotland Yard had let Rodríguez be killed under their noses. The colonel had returned from leave, and had said atrocious things when Galera had suggested that a visit to London by the Jefe de Servicio would help to induce the wholehearted collaboration of the Metropolitan Police.

Prieto was indignant and ironical by turns. Had enough money not been wasted already in dealing with the affairs of idle and corrupt foreigners? Had the telephone service broken down (evidently it had not, from the use to which it had been put in his absence), was the Spanish postal service not the most efficient in Europe, that Galera should think it necessary to involve the state in the expense of a visit to a country politically feeble, in matters of religion wickedly atheistic, and in the conduct of police investigation so inefficient that anarchists were able with impunity to put bombs in the doorways of government ministers? Some people, Prieto said, might see some political implication in Galera's eagerness to visit such a country, but for himself he would only say that the jefe was lacking in judgment. If the Jefe de Servicio had to be interested in foreigners, why not extend his interest to the group of five British students known to have attended a meeting of the Anarcho-Syndicalists in Valencia last week, not one of whom had been arrested? It was as well, Prieto said, that he had returned, for even though this political matter was not the direct responsibility of the DIC, it was right to be concerned about it.

Galera resigned himself, bowed like a sapling in the wind. Farewell, Scotland Yard. Farewell, Rose and Crown, Golden Lion, Goat and Compasses, and all those other places with wonderful names. Progress on the case slowed to nothing, the exchange of correspondence. Then he learned with astonishment about the substitution of the dental chart, which seemed to show that the body washed up had been that of the man Summers, to whose disappearance he had paid little attention. Rider was still alive, and perhaps had not even left Spain. He found the affair incomprehensible yet fascinating, but the colonel so clearly considered time spent on it to be time wasted that Galera did not dare do more than put out a description of Rider, with a request that any man answering this description should be detained. This led to one or two wild-goose chases, including an unfortunate incident when a visiting English priest was detained in Saragossa. The colonel was heavily sarcastic. The case languished.

Until the discovery made by Jaime and Pedro's dog.

North of Valencia is the orange-growing country, and Jaime and Pedro were the eight-year-old twin sons of a farmer in this district. The dog's name was Silencio, which means in English "silent," and the name was appropriate because he never barked.

The dog belonged to the boys, something a little unusual in Spain, where animals are kept for use rather than as pets. Jaime and Pedro had bicycles, and on a Saturday morning they took a picnic to the Río Selva. The attraction of this particular river was that it held enough water to splash about in even in summer. It was also supposed to contain fish, although the boys had never caught any. Silencio came with them, as he always did, keeping up with the bicycles without apparent effort.

Jaime and Pedro were in the river when they heard the sound. It was not a bark nor exactly a howl, but it contained something of both. It faded as though the barker or howler had been strangled, then was renewed with greater anguish. Could it be that he had found his voice in the moment of being attacked? When they had scrambled out the boys found no attacker, but simply the dog digging frantically at a patch of rough grass some twenty feet from the road down which they had come. Every few seconds he would break off to throw back his head and make this unearthly sound. Then he went back to digging.

When Jaime and Pedro saw what Silencio was digging up, they looked at each other, and then made for their bicycles. The dog followed them, but reluctantly, stopping several times on the way back to give his agonized yowl. The boys' father telephoned the Guardia Civil.

The grave in which the body lay was very shallow, not much more than a covering of earth, and it had remained undiscovered only because few people stopped their cars at this spot. The body was that of a large man, and the cause of death was immediately apparent. He had been shot through the head. The man was fully clothed, and at the mortuary in Valencia his clothing was examined. The contents of his wallet appeared to be intact. They belonged to Roger Rider.

Manuel Galera's immediate reaction was one of skepticism. It was not possible to get prints from the corpse's fingers, and no dental identification could be made because Rider's original dental card had been destroyed. His medical record, however, still existed. It gave information about an appendectomy scar and about a fracture of the left leg which had mended imperfectly. When he learned that the corpse showed the same scar and fracture, Galera acknowledged that the body was that of Rider. The discovery deepened his depression. The pathologist was unable to say more than that the man had certainly been dead for some weeks. The obvious assumption was that he had been killed on the night of his disappearance, but if this was so, the times and distances made it impossible for Geoffrey Paradine to have been concerned. And if Rider had left the corrida deliberately, remained in hiding afterward and been killed at some later date, Paradine had again to be left out of consideration, for by this time he was back in England.

There were many subsidiary problems. If Rider was himself a victim, who had killed Summers, and presumably Hubert Paradine as well? And what need had there been for Rodríguez to die? Galera became obsessed by the case. He was upset by the English newspapers, which had headings like "Missing Tycoon Found in Spanish Ravine" and "Mystery of Holiday Deaths" and went on to imply that the Spanish police had shown little enthusiasm about solving the case from the start. Reporters came out from England, and asked questions along these lines. He wanted to tell them that his own enthusiasm and interest had been frustrated by the stupidity and short-sightedness of his superiors, but regard for his job compelled him to refrain. Most maddening of all was the colonel's attitude. With the interest aroused by the discovery of the body, and the news stories sent back by reporters who linked the deaths under headings like "The Strange Happenings at Villa Victoria," the colonel himself was jerked into action by the general in Madrid. From complaining that Galera's interest was a waste of time, the colonel had turned to demanding results. He expressed astonishment that with all the time spent on the affair, not a single person had yet been detained. He had the nerve to suggest, without actually stating it as a fact, that if he had been present and in charge himself, everything would have been cleared up. He knew, he said, that Galera did not interest himself in politics, but had he considered the possibility that this was a political matter? Did Rider or some member of his party have a connection with the Spanish Communist Party, the Maoists, the Trotskyists, the Democratic Students . . . ?

All this nonsense made Galera short-tempered. At home María felt the thwack of his belt, used not in play but in earnest. At the office he took refuge in studying the thick file on his desk. Since it seemed likely that Rider had left Valeta alive on the night of his disappearance, how had he done it? Galera found himself looking at the early reports made before the DIC's involvement, with more care than he had previously given to them. He talked again to Suarez, who had investigated Rider's movements on that last evening, and then to Ernesto Vara, the clerk who had seen a man resembling Rider picked up on the road just outside Valeta. The incident now took on a new importance, and he had Vara brought in for questioning. Before he did so he had a check made on the clerk, with interesting results.

"You are not a Spaniard," he said to the man who sat on the opposite side of the desk. Vara was small, pockmarked, nervous. But many people were nervous under interrogation by the DIC.

"Pardon?"

"Your father was Brazilian."

"With respect, I was born in Spain. I am a Spaniard."

"Not of Spanish blood." He tapped the papers in front of him. "It is not to be expected that those of foreign blood should feel toward the Caudillo as a Spaniard does."

Vara was sweating. "With respect, my jefe, I am a loyal Spaniard."

"Some of the post-office workers in our province ask for more pay. You support them?"

"Those of us with families find it difficult to live. For the single man it is not so bad."

"*Not so bad.* You mean, even for them it is not good? The Caudillo is the father of his people. Do you think he does not know that we have difficulties, that his ministers do not inform him? Perhaps you think you know better than the ministers?" Vara stared back at him, but said nothing. "You have attended meetings at the house of Armando Carella?"

"Two only, my jefe."

"This Carella is one of those who say we should have more freedom, that we are not democratic. Do you want more democracy? Perhaps you would like to live somewhere else? In England perhaps?" With painful clarity he saw the swing doors of an English pub saying *Saloon Bar*, the back-slapping friendliness within. He hardly listened to Vara saying that he hoped only for a little more money and had stopped attending the meetings at Carella's house as soon as he understood that they were a group trying to change the laws, that he was a faithful Spaniard and would not wish to live in any other country. Vara was obviously harmless, and all this had been merely a softening-up process. A process, incidentally, that would be baffling to Vara, who would know that if this were a serious political matter he would have been interrogated by the Guardia Civil.

"On the night of September seventh you attended one of Carella's meetings."

"It was the last time. Since then I swear I have not—"

"Save your breath. I am not interested in your connection with Carella, although I advise you to avoid him in future. On that evening you saw a car stop, and a man get into it. I want you to tell me everything about what happened then."

Vara stared. "I have told already all I remember."

"We shall see. Perhaps there is something you forgot. First of all, the car. Its color?"

"Green."

"What color green? Like that of the Guardia uniform? No. Darker than that or lighter? A bright shining green or a dull one?"

"Not exactly any of those. The color was not precisely green, more like that stone—what is it? A turquoise. A greeny blue, more like a turquoise than an emerald."

"Was all the car this color?" Vara hesitated. "Think, man. It is important."

The clerk closed his eyes, opened them again. "It was two colors of green. The roof was one color, brighter. The rest of the car a greeny blue. I saw it under a street lamp—the color might be changed in daylight."

"But two colors, you are sure? Good. That was something you had not remembered. Now, a new car or an old?"

"Not old. Perhaps almost new."

"The make?"

"I do not know, I have no interest. On a post-office clerk's salary—"

"Look at these, tell me which shape is most like the car you saw." He had had a dozen outline shapes prepared. Vara chose a Mercedes, but with some hesitation. He had no recollection of the number, but after five minutes' interrogation said that he thought it had a Valencia number plate.

Galera was pleased. He offered Vara a beer, drank one himself. Gómez would not have approved of this civilized treatment. "You see that the tales they tell about us are not true," he said jovially. "They say we knock people about. Instead we give them beer. If you were in London they would not offer you beer, I can tell you."

Vara smiled nervously. "I have never been out of Spain. I never wish to be."

"Spain is the place to live. But England is not so bad. They drink beer from the wood, as they call it, not in cans. Excellent." Both men belched. "Now, back to business. Tell me just what happened when this man was picked up. Everything, you understand. The man who was picked up, did he stand there waiting? Did you see him first?"

"No. First the car stopped in the road. I was walking toward it. It stopped perhaps twenty meters from me. I went on walking, and I passed it. After I had gone past I saw this man walking toward it, again a few meters away. He was on the other side of the road from me, hurrying a little, not running but walking quickly, and I looked round to see if the car had stopped for him. It had. He opened the door, got in. The car drove away."

"Very good." Galera beamed, as at a promising pupil. "Let us see what else you remember. The driver?"

"I am not sure. I did not look specially."

"You said he was about your own age."

"Did I? I am not certain even of that. He was not an old man, not fifty. And he was dark, not fair."

"A Spaniard?"

"Perhaps. Like myself."

"Clothes?"

"I do not remember. I am almost sure he was not wearing a jacket, that is all."

"Tall or short?"

"He was in the driver's seat, how could I tell?"

Galera nodded. He had asked the question only to see if Vara was inventing details. "And the other man?"

"Big, taller than me, much bigger altogether. Gray hair. I have said this already."

"Clothes?"

"Some sort of bright shirt, trousers, espadrilles."

"No jacket?"

"He may have been carrying a jacket. I think he was."

Galera nodded again. A jacket had been found in the grave, and the other clothes corresponded well enough. He produced a photograph of Rider, a much better one than the snapshot Vara had been shown already, and asked whether that was the man. The clerk would say no more than that it could have been.

A blue-green car with a top of a different color, fairly new, probably a Mercedes, a Valencia number plate. It was his idea to try at once the care-hire and taxi firms, his idea also to concentrate on the smaller firms, on the basis that if the man who picked up Rider was a hired assassin, he would probably have used a small firm rather than a large one. His hunch was right. A garage proprieter named Ramón Ortega, who ran a little car-hire business on the side, had rented just such a car to an Englishman on the afternoon of September 7. The car was a Mercedes, and had been hired on a daily basis, but when Ortega opened up the garage on the following morning he had found the car outside in the street, and the Englishman had never turned up again. Ortega had not minded this, because there was nothing wrong with the car and he retained the deposit.

What was the man like? Medium height, dark and bearded, wearing a lightweight dark suit. About forty years old, his hair and beard streaked with gray. He spoke a little Spanish, not much, and they had hardly any conversation. Did he have a driving license? Ortega was indignant: of course he had an International Driving License. He showed Galera the form that the man had signed. There was the name, in a backward-sloping hand: *Martin Meacham.*

There was one other possibility that Galera followed up. To bury a body, even in a shallow grave, some implement would have been needed. He had inquiries made at the leading hardware stores in Valencia, and to his surprise one detective found a shop assistant who remembered selling a spade to a bearded Englishman. The assistant could not be sure of the date, but he remembered the sale because he spoke some English, which he was anxious to air. He had said to the man: "You will be using this to dig up your garden?" and he remembered the man's laughing reply: "No, to bury a body." The remark had seemed to the shop assistant not in good taste.

The purchase of the spade left no doubt about the premeditated nature of the crime. It looked as though Meacham was a man hired to come over from England to kill Rider. An examination of flight records showed that a passenger, M. Meacham, had flown to Valencia from Heathrow, arriving at three o'clock on Saturday the seventh, and that he had taken the first flight back on Sunday morning. At that point the trail ended. There was no

Martin Meacham in British passport records, so that presumably the name was invented and the passport forged.

Galera gave an interview to one of the British newspapermen, in which he talked about the tracing of the car and the spade, with which he was rather pleased. "The killer came from England. Rider died in this country, but the origin of this horrific crime is deep in the roots of his English affairs."

"What about the other body, the one you thought was Rider at first? It doesn't look as though this Meacham was here when *he* was killed, does it?"

"I have no comment."

"And how about Scotland Yard? Have they given you the collaboration you expect?"

"They have been in every way superb." And it was true that Galera had had many telephone conversations with Lawton, and that they were on Christian-name terms. Carried away by this thought, he went on. "It may still be necessary for me to visit England and continue there the search for the mysterious Meacham. I do not rule it out."

"You think he's in England?"

"I am not sure of it."

The story appeared under the heading: "WHERE IS MYSTERY MAN MARTIN MEACHAM?" and began: "Jefe de Servicio Manuel Galera of Spain's famed DIC (he wears no uniform, but his rank is that of a Major) rapped the desk between us and said: 'Martin Meacham, the mystery man we are looking for, is in England, I am sure of it. I expect to fly over to continue the search for him. . . .' "

When the colonel read this he was not pleased. Galera gave no more interviews to British press men, and within another week the press had lost interest in the case. At Scotland Yard, Lawton kept Feathers in touch with all these developments, but the superintendent saw nothing in them to revive his own interest. In Spain, Galera insisted that nothing further could be done there, but he was still denied his trip to England. Then a case in which an unsuccessful attempt was made to kill a woman through an electrical device in the bathroom came his way, and he was quickly absorbed in trying to show that it was not her husband but her mother who had fixed the wires to the towel rail. He was discomfited some weeks later when the culprit proved to be the woman's ten-year-old son, but by that time the case of Roger Rider was over.

PART FOUR | The Plot
Against
Roger Rider

1

"Why you ever thought you were queer is more than I can imagine," Sheila said. She had moved into the flat, and they were lying in bed together. "You've no need to worry about that."

"It wasn't a question of worrying. Everybody's queer, more or less. It was just a question of which it was, whether it was more. Or less."

"Very much less, I should say."

"Instead of talking so much about the Natural Man, why don't you behave like a Natural Woman?"

"How do you mean?"

"Make some breakfast."

She went obediently to the kitchen, which was still in the chaotic condition of Jerry's day, with dirty plates in the sink and saucepans containing unidentifiable fragments of food on the draining board. It occurred to her that the Natural Woman was probably sluttish, and that the desire for order was no doubt a late development. She found clean cups and plates, put them on a tray, made toast and coffee. When she took them into the living room James was on the floor in his dressing gown, with his legs crossed, reading a book.

"About the Natural Woman. Don't you think the instinct for order is a late development, especially for women? I mean there's no proof, is there, that man has a natural tendency to build? So why should we think that woman has a natural tendency to make a home, keep things clean and tidy—"

He looked up. "What?"

She poured coffee. "You might at least pretend to listen to me."

"Sorry. Do you know what's just occurred to me? Meacham has used the same trick as Chesney. Or Merrett. Almost the same, anyway."

"James, I just don't know what you're talking about."

"Sorry," he said again. When he looked up and smiled she felt that painful and pleasurable twanging sensation somewhere inside. "I'm becoming Obsessional Man. This was a real case. Donald Merrett killed his mother up in Edinburgh when he was eighteen, but managed to get away with it. Later he changed his name to Chesney and carried on all sorts of rackets. He was living in Germany, and he wanted to kill his wife, who was in London."

"Why did he want to kill her?"

"For the insurance. The point is this. Chesney was the obvious suspect. So he worked out an alibi for himself in Germany, and then flew over to England using a false passport. He did his killing and flew back. As Chesney he'd never been out of Germany."

"Obviously he didn't get away with it, or you wouldn't be telling the story. How did they catch him?"

"He had the bad luck to meet his wife's mother on the stairs, so he killed her too, and left a lot of clues."

She spread a bit of toast with marmalade. "So what? I don't see that gets you any further. I mean, we know Meacham used a forged passport."

"Yes, but suppose he was creating an alibi. Suppose there was somebody in England who wanted to kill Rider, and was known to have a motive, so that he'd be an obvious suspect. This way he's safe—" His voice trailed away, as he saw the fallacies in what he was saying.

"Drink your coffee, it may help you to think straight," Sheila said unkindly. "What you're saying doesn't make sense. Your

Chesney had an alibi when the body was found. But Meacham tried to *hide* the body—don't you think there's something horrible about him going out and buying the spade? Then when it was found, the police discovered quite quickly that he'd been using a forged passport. So the most likely thing is still that he was a killer hired by someone, who just went out and did a job."

"Another bright idea gone wrong." He sat with bowed head and slumped shoulders. It was because he looked so dejected, and she wanted to cheer him up, that she made what turned out to be a vital remark. "Anyway, you're obviously right, and there was some sort of plot against daddy."

"But then he was arranging the plot himself, wasn't he? The plot to disappear and leave my father as suspect for his murder." He stared at her. "That's it, don't you see? There were *two* plots against Roger Rider."

He unfolded his legs, knocking his coffee cup over on its side. A thin trickle of coffee went onto the carpet. She got up, fetched a cloth from the kitchen and wiped up the coffee, wondering as she did so why she didn't leave him to do it himself when he had spilled the coffee. And why did it give her this obscure feeling of satisfaction to do it? She caught up with what he had been saying.

"It was all laid out before us, only we couldn't see it. The first plot was Rider's own. We know all about that. He's up to his neck in trouble. If he just disappears he'll have Interpol looking for him on fraud charges. He's got to die. So he evolves this plan which makes it look as though he's dead and as though my father has killed him. He knows about Amanda's affair, and deliberately highlights this by getting in touch with that private detective. Since dad was besotted with Amanda, Rider could rely on it that dad would come out to Spain. Rider's already arranged for Summers to be there, and Rodríguez must have worked for him before. The plan is to kill Summers, keep him till he's unrecognizable, then release the body, identified by the dental chart. Who killed him? Answer, Geoffrey Paradine."

"Suppose the body wasn't washed up?"

"It wouldn't matter too much. Rider'd have disappeared, and there'd be a strong presumption that he was dead. Did he say anything to you about all this on that car journey out there?"

"In a way perhaps he did. He said we were all forced to do things we didn't want to do. And there was something about living dangerously. I thought he was talking about being a tycoon. He was fond of me in a way, you know. And I liked him. It's hard to imagine him being so—so devious."

"Remember that he was desperate."

"I suppose so." She sighed. "It's hard to know what anybody's like really, isn't it?"

He ignored this. "Then things went wrong. Uncle Hubert realized that your father was intending to disappear anyway, and turned up to make it clear that he'd have to be paid out, threatening your father through the game we played. After that your father went off for a walk, remember? I think he went to find Summers and tell him that he wanted help. While the rest of us were sleeping soundly because we'd been doped, they took Hubert out in his car and tipped him over into that ravine. Probably Rodríguez went with them too. Talking of horrible touches, they must have dressed Hubert and packed his sleeping things in his case—that's macabre, if you like. And it was curtains for Summers too, though he didn't know it. One or the other of them hit and stunned him, and Rodríguez went out that night and tied him to the buoy. Unexpected hitch disposed of, operation all according to plan. The next night Rider disappears, also according to plan. He must have expected to be taken out of the country, en route to wherever his money was stashed away. Then the body of Summers is eventually released, and my father's the obvious suspect when the body's thought to be Rider. And that was the end of Roger's own plot."

"What was the other plot, then?"

"A real one against him, separate from the one he'd faked up."

"You don't have any proof of it, do you?"

"Only through things that Jerry said before he took off. And the fact that a lot of people are dead. And that it makes sense."

"What about Rodríguez getting killed?"

"He was like Uncle Hubert, trying to cash in on what he knew."

"But who killed him?"

"The person he was blackmailing."

"If there's one thing more infuriating than another, James Paradine, it's that smug air of superiority—"

"All right," he said hastily. "It's obvious, Amanda."

"But—"

"She must have been in on it from the start. The affair with dad must have been part of Rider's own plan."

She stared at him. "I don't believe it. You mean he *agreed* to it. Oh, that's disgusting."

"It's happened before. It can't have been news to him that she'd been unfaithful."

She wrinkled her nose. "I can see she might have thought it 'amusing,'—that would have been her word. But you're not telling me that she killed my father. She was at the villa when he disappeared. And I can't see her hitting you on the head. It's somehow— I just can't see it."

"I agree. I think she arranged it."

"Who with?"

"With Meacham."

"And who was Meacham?"

"It must have been somebody at BMS, somebody who knew Rider was intending to disappear. And from what Jerry told me, there's only one person who fits the bill. A man who had a lot to lose if BMS packed up, who knew Rider had been cheating, the man Jerry said treated him like dirt. Alastair Stephenson."

2

James's final discoveries in relation to the plot against Roger Rider came through a series of telephone calls. The first of these was to his father. He had decided that the affair ought to be traced right through to its origins, and the origin of his father becoming a suspect had been the report to Jerry by a girl in Foreign Sales that there was something wrong about the way in which the department worked. When James got through, Geoffrey Paradine came on the line loud, clear and uncharacteristically confident.

"How's the book going?" It proved to be a rash question. James listened for what seemed like several minutes to an account of misadventures in his father's childhood which sounded like fragments of any other childhood. Perhaps it would seem more impressive read than heard. He broke in.

"Dad, there's a question I'd like you to answer. About the office. Do you remember a girl who worked in your department, I think her name was Vickers? I suppose she'd have been a clerk of some kind. She either left of her own accord or was sacked, not long ago."

A pause. Then his father said deliberately, "No."

"Perhaps I've got the name wrong. It began with V, though— Vincent, Viner, something like that. And it had two syllables. I want to get in touch with her. You must remember."

"There's no question of *must*. I *don't* remember anybody with that name or anything like it." His voice took on a melting, sentimental tone. "As far as I'm concerned, you must understand, that's all finished. Now I only want to learn, my boy, about the non-existent man of the past."

James prayed God to give him patience and asked a few more questions, but without result. He rang up BMS, spoke to the

Accounts Department, said that his name was Gavin of Mulholland, Gavin and Payne, solicitors, and that he was trying to trace a Miss Vickers in the Foreign Sales Department in connection with a car accident of which she had been a witness. He was told that nobody with a name that began with V had ever been employed in Foreign Sales. After a few minutes' thought he came up with a solution to her non-existence, which he communicated to Sheila.

"She must have been a deliberate plant by your father on Jerry, a way of alerting the police to the idea that there was something wrong in the Foreign Sales Department." Later it occurred to him that another explanation was possible, and he made some more telephone calls. He emerged from them greatly shaken.

That evening Sheila started on the tidying up of the flat that they had been talking about for days. Saucepans were scoured, plates smeared with fat cleaned and made to sparkle, large pockets of dust and cobwebs removed. They turned to Jerry's bedroom. Although he had kept his promise to dispose of everything important, he had left a pile of old clothing and another pile of books and magazines, which were to go to a jumble sale or the Red Cross. James, never one to ignore books and papers, settled down with these while Sheila whirled round with a vacuum cleaner.

"Wells, Henty, *Treasure Island.* Jerry never emerged from a schoolboy taste in reading, you know that? Pamphlets on police procedure—I suppose we shouldn't put them in the jumble. Travel pamphlets, Costa Brava, Normandy and Brittany—never met anyone who had so many travel pamphlets. Italian Riviera, come to Yugoslavia and see glorious Dubrovnik, come to Sardinia and see the nuraghi." He paused, went on more slowly. "The nuraghi, found only in this part of Italy. These centuries-old buildings, made from huge stone blocks, whose origins are still unknown. Et cetera. Turn that thing off a minute, will you?"

"What?"

"Turn that bloody thing off." When she had done so, he waved the pamphlet. "Nuraghi in Sardinia. Mean anything to you?" She shook her head. "Shangri-La. Remember the game that evening. About Amanda's Shangri-La?"

"That was just airy talk."

"Then Roger said he'd provided it. And out there she could solve the mysteries of the nuraghi. Remember how she looked then? I wonder." He sat slapping the brochure against his palm.

On the following morning he rang his father again, and found him slightly querulous. James must remember, he said, that when one was writing, constant interruptions were not helpful.

James broke in. "Sorry, dad. I don't want to keep you from the non-existent man. Just one question. Do you know the name of Rider's secretary, the one who'd deal with his personal affairs?"

"Of course I do. Mary Provine. I've known her for years. That's very different from talking about people who never worked in my department."

James rang BMS, and again invoked Mr. Gavin. He tried to produce what he thought of as a proper legal voice, one that blended oil and vinegar like salad dressing, with the vinegar slightly predominating, a French dressing undoubtedly.

"Miss Provine, I am acting for Mrs. Amanda Rider, whom I think you know, in relation to the estate."

"Yes, I know Mrs. Rider." The voice, middle-aged and cautious, accepted his identity without seeming impressed by it.

"A small query has arisen in relation to the Italian property, which she thought you might be able to help us solve."

"The Italian property?"

He held his breath. Was she going to deny any knowledge of an Italian property? But her next words showed that his logic, or what Sheila would have called his luck, held.

"It's registered in Mrs. Rider's name. I don't know what problem there could be." The voice was sharp. Obviously, Miss Provine had not approved of that registration. A little more oil perhaps?

"The Italian side are being very difficult. They can really be a headache, I can assure you, Miss Provine. People who say English lawyers are time-wasters can never have dealt with Italians." A chuckle, not too dry. Was he overdoing it? No, the ghost of an answering chuckle came back down the line.

"What did you want to know?"

"It's a ridiculous point, a matter of the exact designation and address."

"Just a moment." When she came back she said, "In all the correspondence it was referred to as Castello Bruncu Spina, in the province of Nuoro." He wrote it down. "Well?"

"I beg your pardon?"

"How does that differ from what the Italians say?"

He pulled himself together. "In some of the papers it has been called a castello and in others a palazzo. Because of the difference there's some argument about the authenticity of the agreement."

"It would serve her right if she lost it. But there isn't that much justice in the world." James gave what he hoped was a dry cough. "I'm sorry. She *is* your client."

"Perfectly all right, Miss Provine. Privately, may I say I appreciate your feelings."

When he had rung off he sat looking at the piece of paper. The Castello Bruncu Spina, he thought. Journey's end.

3

To the tourists who swim, water-ski or merely laze every summer on Sardinia's beaches, the idea of bandits holding up their cars seems a good joke. In the mountain areas of the northeast it is another matter. Here nobody has any doubt about the reality of the banditi. The Sards do not talk about them, but they remember the fate of the Townleys, an innocent but over-curious middle-aged couple who were shot and killed on the outskirts of Orgosolo because they insisted on taking photographs of a young man with a rifle, and the affair of the Dutch journalist who rashly tried to drive away from the three masked men who stopped him on the road, and ended up in hospital shot in the shoulder. The bandits are real enough, although the Sards take pride in the fact that they act as individuals and not as an organization. The Mafia belongs to Sicily. In Sardinia, banditry is personal, one of the country's legends.

The Castello Bruncu Spina belongs to these legends. John Warre Tyndale, the Victorian traveler who produced what is in many ways still the finest survey of the island, wrote of the castle with uncharacteristically romantic fervor, as "a dream or a mirage, quivering between earth and sky." From the time of its building in the sixteenth century, the Castello was the home of bandit chiefs, most of them belonging to the Ramini family, whose origins were in Orgosolo. They lived in it until after World War I, when Giuseppe Ramini, after the deaths of his parents, left Sardinia for the mainland of Italy and sold the Castello to an eccentric Englishman named Spate. Some legends cluster thickly about the castle in this period. Spate was a rich man who dabbled in archeology, and was interested in the nuraghi, the strange buildings made of stone blocks that are relics of some megalithic civilization. But his eccentricity had a more sinister flavor. He had mistresses who came to live in the Castello. It was said that orgies took place, that some of the women did not leave the Castello alive, that when Spate died after falling from a wall in a drunken stupor, strange marks were found burned on his arms and chest. The place lay empty for years before Spate's executors sold it to a rich American who had never seen it. He paid one visit, gave instructions for the installation of a lighting plant, modern drainage and new furnishings, and died before the work was completed. It was a long time after his death that the English millionaire or his woman bought it.

Some of this was known only vaguely to the villagers of Fonni and Desulo. Only the oldest of them remembered the Castello being occupied, and when the lorries came out from Nuoro, some bringing beds, tables and cooking things, and others with work-men who repaired walls and floors, they still did not believe that any person in his right mind would come to live there. They had a saying: "Many visit Bruncu Spina, but only the dead stay," and when the Englishwoman came and stayed, there were some who believed she must be dead. For a woman to come alone to such a place showed that she must be either one of the dead or else a witch. When she was seen driving along the road to Nuoro, it was thought that she would not return. She came back, however, and brought with her He-who-was-swathed-in-bandages.

It was said by the devout that this was some kind of sacred relic propped up like a mummy in the seat beside her and swathed in bandages from head to toe, so that only the eyes looked out from the pure white wrappings. Others said that only the face was bandaged, and others still that when the bandages were removed the body was raw as that of a plucked chicken. Those village women who worked at the Castello came back before nightfall, and the men returned also except only Giuseppe, the wild son of the shepherd Giuseppe. He went up to work for the witch in the Castello, and did not return the same evening. When he came back he told tales of the money the witch had given him, and of a room in which He-who-was-swathed-in-bandages was shut away.

James Paradine flew in to Alghero. There he hired a car and drove to Nuoro, where he hoped that somebody would tell him how to reach the Castello Bruncu Spina. The road was broad and good, one of the new autostrade linking the large towns. In Nuoro, which is built on a hill, the wind blew hard, not cold but powerful. The young man at the travel bureau pulled at his lip, shook his head.

"You don't know where it is?"

"I do not know the Castello, I know Bruncu Spina." He led the way across to a map on the wall. "You see here where it says Monti del Gennargentu. These are the highest mountains in our country. And now here, you see, it says La Marmora, and here

Bruncu Spina. You see? Those are the highest peaks. At this time snow will be covering them."

"That's where the Castello will be?"

"As to that, I cannot tell you. I have not heard of it. But, signor, it is not a good place to be. You understand, it is in the mountains. And you are traveling alone."

"I have a friend who lives there. Where could I find out the exact location of the Castello?"

The young man shrugged. "Perhaps in Fonni, perhaps in Desulo."

Two or three miles out of Nuoro the road began to rise, and the rise became steeper as he went on. He had been surprised by the green freshness of the scenery, but as he climbed, evergreen oaks and chestnut trees gave way to gray rock. Within the car it was warm. Outside it the wind blew, whistling through the trees.

He reached Fonni, gray and silent, in early afternoon. He was suddenly aware of feeling hungry, but the village had no restaurant or hotel. He ate ham, cheese and bread, washed down by rough red wine, in a taverna. Three men were in the taverna drinking, no more than an occasional word muttered between them. The proprietor was a thin man with a great curved nose like a bird's beak. When James asked in halting Italian for the Castello Bruncu Spina the men stared at each other. The proprietor took James to the door, pointed along the road to Desulo and set his hand in a steep upward curve.

From Fonni still the road climbed and narrowed. The turns became sharper. In places the road was little more than a track cut through sheer rock. A man stood in the road beside a tiny stone hut, and gazed at the car with what seemed unmistakable hostility. A bandit? James waited for the man's companions to spring out from behind the hut, but at the last moment the man stepped aside and spat. The spittle reached the side window. A couple of minutes later James came to the village.

It was no more than a cluster of houses clinging to the mountain. On one side the land dropped, and he saw what must be

Desulo in the valley below. Above the village there was to be seen only rock and shale, sharply rising. He pulled the car in close to the mountainside and got out. In the doorway of one cottage a woman stood, wearing the red bolero and white blouse of the district. The fierceness of her stare as he approached was not diminished by the fact that she was wall-eyed.

"Per favore, signora," he said. "Conosce la strada per Castello Bruncu Spina?"

She gave him a long deliberate stare, then went in and closed the door. He returned to the car and looked at the map he had bought in Nuoro. It seemed that the mountain named Bruncu Spina must be near. Perhaps, even, this was the mountain, and if the village in the valley was Desulo he would be wasting time in going down there. He had made up his mind to try two or three more houses, when he heard the tinkling of a bell. A moment later a herd of thin athletic-looking sheep came around the bend of the road. The shepherd followed them. James got out of the car again and repeated his question.

The shepherd was a young man, dark and short like many Sards, and he smelled of sheep. He too gave James a long look, but, unlike the woman, he answered.

"Bruncu Spina." He waved his arm around and pointed upward. Evidently this was the mountain. James nodded.

"Castello?"

The man crossed himself, then said, "Castello a destra." He made a gesture indicating that it was up the mountain. When James asked how far it was, he did not reply but turned back to his sheep.

A quarter of a mile out of the village a dirt track led away to the right. He stopped the car. To the left a panorama stretched before him, the road winding down to the village below. Should he go along the road, or turn to the right now? He took the car up the track. The soil on either side had been eroded by rain, and it occurred to him that meeting another car would be far from pleasant. Then he came to a place where it widened a little. Great rocks rose above it, with tiny blue flowers among them. The sky had become dark.

A hairpin bend, and the dirt road gave way to a rocky surface. The car bumped round another hairpin bend. The view opened up, and he saw Bruncu Spina crowned with snow. He also saw the Castello.

It was not truly a castle but a kind of fort, gray and forbidding, perched on the top of its own small separate crag, the mountain towering above it. He drove on another few yards and came to a sheltered spot where concrete had been laid. A small car and a Land-Rover stood here; a path between the rocks led upward. Beyond this point you went on foot, or perhaps by mule. He bent his body into the wind, and started to walk up. It was part walk, part scramble among the rocks, while the wind pulled at his clothing. The track moved round, not directly up, and at one point he lost sight of the Castello altogether. When he saw it again he was much nearer, near enough to see the slits in the walls out of which guns had once pointed, but which were now incongruously juxtaposed with plate-glass windows.

When he stopped to catch his breath he was aware of steps hurrying down the track. In a moment two women in red and white appeared, kerchiefs pulled over their heads. The one in front screamed when she saw him. Both stopped, crossed themselves. Then they made a concerted rush which took them past him and almost knocked him over. Round the next bend he met somebody else, a darkly handsome youth who wore an elaborately frilled red silk shirt and bell-bottom trousers. The young man came bounding over the rocks, shouting something as he passed. Then he had gone, and there was only the crying of the wind.

Another turn, and James was at the entrance. Iron gates confronted him, a courtyard beyond them. He wondered what he would do if the gates were closed, but they opened at a push.

In the courtyard he was out of the wind. The building extended on three sides round it, a long central block with two wings. In each block there was a door. He opened the door in the right-hand side, and went in. It was dark. He found a switch, and a rather dismal illumination appeared.

He was in a scullery that led to the kitchen, and work seemed to have been abandoned during the preparation of a meal. Tomatoes and cucumber had been sliced for a salad, a leg of lamb lay beneath a net, potatoes and onions were peeled for cooking. There was no sound except a steady ticking, which proved to come from a lighting plant housed in its own room just off the kitchen. Why was there so little sound of wind? He crossed to the window over the kitchen sink and found the answer. Double glazing had been put in. Out of the window in this kitchen, which might have come from Hampstead or Highgate, there was the most astonishing view of the mountain. Bruncu Spina towered above this little fortress, ominous and powerful, its peaks like a jagged row of snowy teeth.

Beyond the kitchen a dining room, the table laid for two. Out of the dining room a corridor that ran along what must be the central structure. Here again darkness and silence. He switched on lights, but did not call out. He opened one of the doors on the right and entered a great drawing room. A log fire burned in a chimney space; heads of boar and deer were on the walls with stuffed eagles and a wildcat. Two great windows ran along almost the whole forty-foot length of the room. He looked out of them and saw hillside partly shrouded in black cloud, above it sunlight and the snowy teeth. On this side one could see no house, no road, nothing to indicate the existence of humanity. What kind of life could one live here? he wondered. How long would it be possible for anybody but a mystic to endure it? A mystic or a voluptuary. He thought he knew what he would find here, yet there was a prickling at the back of his neck. It was an effort to turn round. But the room was empty.

He went out again to the corridor. The humming of the electric-light plant was faintly audible. Otherwise silence was total, as it is never total in a city, or even in a countryside where the rustling of trees and grasses is never totally absent. When he called out "Hello" the word reverberated back at him. For the first time it occurred to him that the Castello might be empty.

The next room was a small bedroom, the bed neatly made, llama rugs on the floor. Now he was in the other angle of the building. He opened the next door.

This room was lighted indirectly by some means which suffused it with a soft pinkish glow. At first he saw nothing but the great circular bed in the center, with the woman lying on it asleep. Then he took in the appurtenances, the thick pale-pink carpet, the erotic pictures, the sunken marble bath at one end of the room. Last of all he looked at the figure in a chair beside the bed, shoulders hunched forward, face swathed in bandages.

The sheets were a darker pink than the carpet. Amanda lay on them naked. She was smiling, and looked at peace. Her head was on one side. Beside it deeper red stained the pink sheet.

Journey's end, James Paradine thought. He said to the figure with the bandaged face, "What's up, Jerry? Plastic surgery?"

In these surroundings it was strange to hear the strong, commonplace London voice. "How the hell did you get here?"

"I suppose in a way I knew as soon as you said you were taking that job in South America. It wasn't like you. You went for the plastic surgery?" Jerry nodded. "Then when I thought back, half a dozen things put me onto it. Your saying what Amanda looked like—how could you have known she was a green-eyed beauty when I never mentioned the color of her eyes in my letters? And when I found Rodríguez's address, went off there and got hit on the head, there was only one other person who knew his address for certain, and that was you. And there was another point. You said you'd got an anonymous phone call, but who'd know the flat number, to ring there and not Scotland Yard? It was Amanda, I suppose?"

"Yes. He went to see her, threatened her. She rang me and said something must be done." From behind the muffling bandages there was amusement in his voice. "I didn't hit you hard."

"But I knew for certain when I found that the Miss Vickers who was supposed to have been worried about what was going on at BMS didn't exist. It didn't make sense for her to be part of Rider's plan, so who could it have been but you? Then I rang the Banco Grande, and found you'd never been offered a job. Where did you get their headed paper from? Stolen?"

"Specially printed. If anybody had written to Buenos Aires I'd arranged a cover. I invented the girl at BMS so that I'd get in on the investigation, know what was happening." He nodded at the bed. "It doesn't matter now, but it was all her idea."

"Let me see how much I've got right. Amanda knew about everything, the plan to disappear, throw suspicion on my father, the whole thing. She was part of Rider's plan. But at the same time she was bored with him. And she wanted his money. Where had he stashed it, by the way?"

"The usual thing, a Swiss account. He'd been fool enough to arrange that either of them could draw on it. Everybody was a fool where she was concerned. And what was she? Just a little tart. Look at all this." His sweep of the hand embraced the pictures, and the ceiling mirror which reflected the figure on the bed.

"How did you meet her?"

"In a club. She used to go out searching for talent. Do you remember my telling you once that I'd found a smashing piece who couldn't get enough of it? That was Amanda."

"You must have known what she was like. I don't see how you could have—"

"Just take it as a fact. We're not all like you."

"She must have told Rider she knew somebody who would help him to get out of Spain. Did she say you were at Scotland Yard?"

"No. We thought it might frighten him off. I was supposed to be a Customs official."

"So you came over as Meacham—who'd know better than a policeman where to get hold of a false passport? And Rider met you outside the village. Where was he coming to?"

"Where d'you think? Here."

"Then you made it plausible that you'd resign. And you got here. What went wrong?"

"The plastic surgery. Something to do with my skin. It lacks something or other." He had been undoing the bandages. When the last of them came off, the face was revealed as puckered with great weals. They ran round the nose, under the eyes, on either side of the neck. The skin was like a patchwork, in some places white and stretched, in others red and almost hanging in folds. The effect was repulsive, unrecognizable as Jerry Maitland. James looked away.

"He said he'd operate again in six months' time and there might be some improvement. Not much, though."

"But he ought to have known—"

"Yes. He was a fool or a crook. Or both." He began to put back the bandages, then dropped them. "What does it matter now? Do you know what happened when I got here? She made me take off the bandages. Then she said I'd turned into a freak, and making love to a freak was interesting, but you wouldn't want to do it more than once. She didn't want to look at me. I had to stay next door while she went to bed with some boy from the village. We'd planned to stay here a few weeks, then live in South America. If you've got enough money, there are places where nobody worries you. But she said she didn't want a freak around, and I was to go out there while she stayed here with Giuseppe. She offered me money—of course she'd kept control of that. As though I'd been in it for money."

"She used you. Like everybody else."

"She won't use anybody again. She was in bed with the boy when I did it." He took a revolver from his pocket, weighed it in his hand.

"Jerry, people know where I am. They'll come looking."

Jerry laughed again. The action puckered up the skin round his mouth, so that he looked like a clown. "You think I'd try anything? What would be the point? And remember, I didn't hit you hard. Anyway, if I'd been going to use it, it would have been on myself. But I'm not the suicidal type."

"Look, Jerry, I'm not a judge, or a policeman, for that matter. If you want to try for South America—"

"With this face? You must be joking. And if I'm not mistaken, the hired help has gone tearing down that breakneck track to tell the local coppers. If you want to be friendly, you might stay with me till they come. There are some cards in the living room."

When the carabinieri arrived, they had just finished their third game of piquet. Jerry had won them all.